Coffee & Cake

Patsy Collins

The author can be found at
www.patsycollins.uk

ISBN: 978-1-914339-07-3

To my friend Maria Christou.

I hope we'll meet for real coffee and cake soon, and that this will give you something to smile about until then.

Contents

1. Birthday Cake

Sam woke from a dream about chocolate cake and fumbled under his pillow to switch off the alarm. He kept it buried there so as not to wake the rest of the household. He pulled it out to check. Yes! He was getting really good at this; there were barely two minutes to go before it would have gone off. It was only during the first few weeks of his paper round that the alarm had gone off and woken him. He didn't really need it any more, but enjoyed beating it by as narrow a margin as possible. Besides, he didn't want to risk oversleeping and letting his boss down.

It was his birthday, but that didn't mean Sam wasn't going to do his job as usual. It was important to him that he was considered reliable.

"I could probably find someone else, if you wanted to take a day off," his boss had offered.

"No, that's fine," Sam had assured him.

He knew he might as well work, no one else would be up for hours yet. He got dressed quietly, knowing he wouldn't disturb Josh in the next room. That kid slept like the dead.

Although he'd never admit it, and although they were the furthest apart in age, seven-year-old Josh was his favourite. They enjoyed the same daft jokes and played football together.

Maybe Sam was biased, but he thought young Josh was a talented player and was looking at ways to get him 'spotted' by someone who could help him develop.

Sam was as quiet as he could be in the bathroom. That was next to Paul and Martha's bedroom. Naturally theirs was the largest. Sam's, having been the guest room until he moved in, was the next biggest. He'd offered to swap it for Josh's box room, but Martha had very kindly talked him out of it.

"We'd need to redecorate it for Josh and besides he's happy where he is. You don't wind it the way it is for now, do you?"

"No, it's very nice." That was true, the soft blue and cream decor was soothing and Sam had come to think of it as his room from his previous visits.

He didn't need to worry about the twins down the hallway. He wouldn't be passing their rooms and they slept just as soundly as their little brother.

"Is there anything special you'd like for your birthday?" Martha had asked a couple of weeks ago.

There was, but he couldn't ask for it. Well he could have, but that wouldn't have been the same thing at all. What Sam wanted was for Martha to make him a big gooey chocolate cake, just as she'd made for each of her boys and her husband on their birthdays.

"I'd like it if we could all have tea together," Sam said, coming as close as he felt he could to mentioning what he wanted.

"Of course. It's a Sunday so that shouldn't be a problem."

Martha's cakes were delicious and Sam was as fond of chocolate as anyone else, but that wasn't the main reason he wanted the cake. He felt that if Martha baked one for him, without any prompting, it would show she truly considered him as part of her family. Martha being the only one he wasn't related to by blood, that felt important.

As Sam took out the milk for the big bowl of crunchy nut cornflakes he fixed himself most mornings, he noticed cream cheese and cress and other things Martha used for family tea parties. That was a good sign. Sam set off to work in an optimistic mood.

A funny birthday card from his boss made Sam smile. He was even more pleased the other delivery lads had contributed to a pack of his favourite sweets.

There were fewer papers to deliver on Sundays, but they were much heavier and the houses they had to go to just as spread out, so the job took almost as long as on the other days of the week. It was a lovely morning though and Sam enjoyed the feeling of having the fresh new day to himself.

As he cycled round the now familiar route he couldn't help thinking about chocolate cake.

He'd moved into his new home just under a year ago, so the family had all had birthdays, and cake, since then. After Josh blew out his candles he'd cut himself a big wedge and left Martha to serve everyone else. The twins had been born one each side of midnight so had separate birthdays and a cake each. Their technique was the same though. They shared the blowing out of candles then cut a reasonable sliced piece for everyone else, reserving a larger chunk for themselves and their twin.

Paul didn't have a candle for each year, but two bigger ones denoting his age of forty-two. He'd cut a normal sized slice for Martha and the barest sliver for everyone else, but had given the game away by his laughter and they all knew they'd get another piece. Martha had no candles on hers. She cut her cake evenly, careful to favour no one. As Sam cycled home he was almost positive she'd bake a cake for him.

The rest of the morning was taken up with opening cards and presents. Everyone sung happy birthday to him, though the twins used the 'squashed tomatoes and stew' version. As they were to have afternoon tea, Martha had suggested they have brunch.

"What's that?" Josh had asked.

"A late breakfast and early lunch all together."

"With sausages and eggs and mushrooms?" Josh asked eagerly, further proving how much he and Sam had in common.

"If that's what everyone would like."

It was.

Afterwards Paul drove them down to the beach for the afternoon where they played football on the sand and flew Sam's new kite. Martha stayed at home. Sam hoped she was baking chocolate cake.

"Up you all go and get washed and changed," she said when they tumbled back into the house. "Tea is ready when you are."

The table was set with plates of sandwiches and sausage rolls, bowls of crisps and a tray of vegetables and dips. There was a teapot and jugs of milk, and orange juice. Right in the centre was a space, just big enough for a cake.

"Oh, looks like I forgot something," Martha said. She went to the kitchen and returned with a chocolate cake.

It wasn't bigger than anyone else's had been, it wasn't better iced and didn't have extra decorations. It was exactly as everyone else's had been and to Sam that made it the very best birthday cake he could have been given.

Martha lit the candles.

"Come on then, Granddad, make a wish and blow them out," Josh said.

Sam took a deep breath and blew out the two candles shaped like a seven and an eight to show his age. He didn't need to make a wish though. Now he knew Martha had meant what she'd said about her being happy to share her home with him as he was family, he had all he wanted.

2. The Perfect Woman

She was there again this morning; the perfect woman. You know the one I mean. She walks past, looking like she's just stepped out of an upmarket salon, the second after you've caught sight of your own reflection in a shop window and realised this is your worst ever bad hair day. She exposes a tiny, tanned midriff on the mornings you finished the kid's toast and are feeling bloated. If you've ripped off yet another nail trying to clean the mud off your loveable, yet daft, dog and your varnish is peeling you'll see her gesturing with a perfect French manicure.

My hair had been sort of OK when I left home, but it'd got rained on and turned frizzy since then. I didn't have a broken nail, but my chapped hands were red and I'd torn a cuticle while sorting the dirty laundry. My stomach wasn't bulging over my jeans, but I was wearing the wrong white top. The one which gapes open between the third and fourth buttons and which has a faint stain on the sleeve. These two facts always seem to go unnoticed until after I've left the house.

I'm not normally one of those woman who feels exposed and vulnerable without makeup, but Ms Perfect sauntered by and I knew I should have found time for applying concealer to the bags under my eyes.

She looked like an advert for something; I wasn't sure what, but I knew it would be expensive. Her outfit looked expensive too. Italian, I guessed. She wore a wide-brimmed hat which framed rather than hid her flawless face. It wasn't there to conceal tatty hair. A few glossy locks artfully escaped. I wasn't sure which were shinier, her shoes, the lipstick on her pouty mouth or the gleam in my husband's eye. I couldn't blame Terry; that seductive wiggle had part hypnotised me too.

What was my husband thinking? Wishing I looked like her? Wishing I was somewhere else. Had he even remembered he had a wife?

"If you're wondering about that hat," I said, "then I don't think it would suit you."

"I suppose not." Terry sounded a little wistful. He looked at me then added, "Not that I'd want it anyway; it wouldn't go with anything I've got."

He pulled at his fleece as he said it, but I guessed he meant more than his clothes.

"Come on, Sally, let's get some shoes on the kids' feet," Terry said and went into the newsagent's, where they'd gone to spend their pocket money, to fetch them.

I waited outside and watched Perfect Woman glide into a coffee shop. She didn't pull the door when she should have pushed or get her handbag caught up with an old lady's brolly. She didn't look as though she felt guilty about not rushing back to do the ironing or as though she was stopping for a special treat.

"Mum, why can't I wear trainers at Auntie Julie's wedding?" My son repeated his well worn plea.

He thought trainers in the same style as Liverpool's goalie were always the ideal footwear.

"Mum, can I have sparkly pink shoes, like a princess?"

I didn't know which of the young royals my daughter was thinking of, but I did know sparkly pink wouldn't go with her yellow bridesmaid dress.

The girl in the shoe shop wasn't another Ms Perfect; she was perfectly wonderful. She knew everything including which type of sensible black shoe was the exact match of the ones the England team wore with those suits they wear to get onto planes. She also had it on good authority that a certain young HRH only ever wore cream shoes. Terry paid before anyone could wonder where she came by her information.

We'd promised the kids they could go to the pictures if they'd been good. Two pairs of shoes in carrier bags in less than an hour and not a single tear or temper tantrum was better than good.

"Would you like to watch the film on your own?" I asked, when I saw our next door neighbour queuing with her own two little darlings.

"Yes!"

"Yeah!"

In exchange for the price of far too much pick and mix than was good for them for all four children, and a promise to be waiting outside when the film finished, Terry and I bought an hour or so of peace.

"What would you like to do?" Terry asked.

"Let's just relax with a coffee?" I suggested. Even as I said it, I realised my motivation had been seeing Ms Perfect an hour earlier and a wish to be a little more like her.

"Yeah, it'll make a nice change to spend a couple of quid on ourselves and just do nothing for a while," Terry said. I'm sure at that point I was the only woman on his mind.

We too managed to get through the door without incident; I might not be accustomed to an easy life, but I'm a quick learner.

"You find a table and look after the shoes, I'll get the drinks... and a cake?" Terry suggested.

As I sat, I noticed Ms Perfect was still there, lingering over her drink. Relaxing, or filling time? Her pointy, blemish-free chin rested on an elegant, long-nailed hand. Her complexion may have owed something to the contents of a pricey bottle, but it seemed the slender figure was real enough. The unopened portion of cream on her saucer and lack of a cake plate suggested that. Black coffee on its own didn't seem such a treat, but maybe that was really how she preferred it. My own choice is for cream, sugar, gateau and someone to share it all with.

Those lovely hands probably never peeled potatoes after a shift in the supermarket. I'm fairly certain of that. It's just a guess that neither did they model colourful dough animals with excited kids. Maybe Perfect Woman wasn't in a hurry because like me she'd be going home to the breakfast things still on the table and a pile of muddy sports-kit strewn around the house, but somehow I doubted it. Maybe she also had a hairy dog to slobber an affectionate welcome and 'love you Mum' notes in wobbly writing taped onto the fridge. That seemed unlikely, but hopefully she had other things which brought her joy. We're all different, aren't we?

Her coffee wouldn't increase the size of her hips, but why be jealous of her slender figure when I had someone to squeeze my love handles? Men admired the way she looked, only one gave me a second glance. That man was at the counter, trying to decide which cake I'd like best and knowing without asking that today I'll be in the mood for coffee in a tall slim mug with a little chocolate powder sprinkled on the top.

Terry placed a loaded tray on the table, making me jump. He'd selected the type of cake that had to be eaten with a fork. Two different kinds so we could try both.

"It wouldn't suit you either, love. The hat," he said.

"Just as well. It wouldn't go with anything I've got."

Who wants to be Ms Perfect when they could be Mrs Slightly Flawed, but perfectly happy?

3. In A Jam

Rose bit into a scone and chewed slowly.

"Is it all right, Miss?" asked a girl whose pigtails still held traces of the flour she'd sifted a little too enthusiastically.

Rose decided she'd kept her class in suspense long enough. "Excellent. All they need now is some strawberry jam." She produced a pot from the very same batch that had won her a red rosette in last year's summer show.

As she watched the children eating their scones, Rose considered the different kind of jam she was in. She loved entering the cookery section classes of the village show. It wasn't just because she often won a prize; it was important to keep traditions going, both of village shows and of making things. Too often people thought that cooking involved opening a packet and slipping something in the oven. Rose liked to bake bread and cakes. She enjoyed making hearty soups from vegetables she'd grown herself. Most of all she loved making preserves. Chutneys, jams, pickles; it didn't matter.

The scent of simmering fruit always made her happy. Rose remembered the delicious smell of her grandmother cooking the same recipes. The first batch of strawberry jam signalled the start of the long summer holidays. Tomato chutney spooned into tall jars meant it was time for her uniform skirt to be let down ready for the new term. It was because of her gran and the recipes she'd passed down that Rose loved making the preserves, and because of her that she now faced a dilemma.

Gran said she was giving up making preserves. The dear lady had trouble reading the recipes and struggled to lift the heavy pans. Gran had recently confided she felt a little left out now she couldn't compete in the show. Rose had teased her that she'd only given up because Rose had beaten her three years running.

Rose's gran had recently bought a trophy to be presented for the best pot of preserves in the show. Gran wouldn't be judging of course, specially trained women were drafted in for that difficult task, but her name would be on the trophy and she'd present it. Bad enough to win a trophy presented by your relation, but even worse when you'd been named for that relation so it was your name too that was engraved on it even before the contest started. It'd be embarrassing to win and might look as though she'd cheated. It might be even more embarrassing not to win. Rose thought she'd better not compete, at least this year, but that option was ruled out as soon as she spoke to Gran.

"About the trophy…" Rose said as she poured Gran a cup of tea.

"Brilliant idea of mine, wasn't it? Now I'm still involved with the show."

"Yes, that is good."

"And I'm really hoping it will attract a few more entries, numbers have been dwindling lately."

They had, and they'd be one less without Rose.

"I remember when I first entered," Gran said. "A Mrs Perkins won every year. I so wanted to beat her that I pestered her for her recipe and I practised and practised, perfecting my techniques until I did."

"I bet she wasn't too happy about that!"

"I thought she'd be disappointed, but she was actually delighted she'd inspired me and quite happy to give up her title for a year."

"Gran, I have a feeling there will be a record number of entries this year," Rose had said.

The sound of children scraping the last sweet traces of strawberry jam from the jar brought Rose back to the present. "Did you like my jam, class?"

"Lovely, Miss. Is there any more?"

"There will be if you make it."

Rose had obtained the headmistress's permission for her class to make jam and enter the competition. The idea was popular and soon the class were teasing each other that they'd be the one with the trophy. Rose instructed the children to ask at home for any family recipes and she was pleased to see several children arrive with old yellowing recipe books, or well used scrapbooks. Some used Rose's gran's traditional recipes, others wanted to try modern versions with reduced sugar or exotic fruits. The headmistress was so impressed with their enthusiasm she bought fruit and sugar for them. Each pupil could select one pot for the competition and the rest would be sold at the show to make money for school projects. Parents and support staff came on the day the jam was made, to help supervise the children as they cooked and transferred the hot preserve into sterile jars.

As Rose predicted, the show received a record number of entries.

Rose won first prize; in the baking class with a loaf of home made bread. She'd be teaching her class to make that in the autumn term.

4. Simple Pleasures

With a frustrated sigh, Jennifer threw down the magazine. Why did everything have to be so complicated? Life used to be simple and fun, but recently it all seemed to be getting on top of her. It wasn't much comfort to know she wasn't the only person to feel that way. Neil had been sympathetic when she'd mentioned it to him.

"I know what you mean, love. Why don't you take the day off on our anniversary and just unwind?"

She'd tried to follow his advice by relaxing with a coffee and the crossword. After she'd chosen from filter coffee, ordinary instant or the decaffeinated kind and realised she'd have to add buying more milk to the day's 'to do' list, she'd sat down. The crossword had proved to be the kind where, as well as working out the answer, she was expected to decide where to put it. That's why the magazine had ended up on the floor, Jennifer had coffee on her skirt and there was a biro mark on the cream leather sofa.

She cleaned the upholstery with the special cleaner and rubbed in some colour restorer, before polishing it back to its former glossy perfection. Jennifer remembered the second, or possibly fifth-hand, sofa that had been their pride and joy when she and Neil had first lived together. It had a multi-coloured throw that didn't show marks and could be washed easily on the rare occasions that seemed necessary. The leather one was nicer she decided before washing her cup, getting changed and setting off to collect the ironing, more milk and her son, Tony, from wherever it was he'd spent the day researching his college project.

Of course Tony couldn't just simply tell her where he was going before he left home and arrange a time to be collected; that would have been far too straightforward.

"I'll give you a call later, Mum."

Jennifer had spent her time relaxing within earshot of the phone and done her unwinding while prepared to drive off to wherever she was summonsed.

Tony had sent her a text message with the postcode of his current location, so she could enter it into her bossily irritating sat-nav, and the time 'they' would require transport. His friends would be needing lifts too and they might all want to go somewhere other than home.

Her whole life seemed to be getting more confusing and less fun. The ironing service was a perfect example. It was supposed to help, but she could probably do the job in less time than it took to battle through the rush-hour traffic after work each week to deliver it. As a bonus there would never be the irritation of realising the item someone wanted to wear wasn't at home. Today it was Neil's dress shirt in the wrong place at the wrong time. Jennifer missed their student days when they'd barely owned enough clothes to make a trip to the laundrette worthwhile and anything without baked beans stuck to the front was considered fit to wear. She grinned as she recalled evenings eating a shared plate of beans curled up together on the sofa wearing only their dressing gowns, and the kissing and cuddling that had occasionally resulted in spilt food.

Jennifer paid and thanked the girl for doing the ironing, put the neatly folded, crease free clothes on the back seat and set off. At the first corner, they slid onto the floor. She didn't bother picking them up when she parked outside the grocers. Tony and his friends would probably move them again anyway. As it was a small shop, the choice of milk was limited. She only had to decide between skimmed, semi-skimmed, full fat or long life and each type only came in three different sizes.

Once, she'd tried shopping on-line, but after an hour all she'd managed to choose was a delivery time and select bread (there were fifty-seven variations on that theme) butter (eighteen options) and the milk. Still, it was good they could now buy whatever they chose to eat. When they'd first been married, they were restricted to whatever they could afford from the limited range in the local shop. Paying bus fare to the bigger shops would have left them with no money to spend when they got there.

Buses! Jennifer had almost forgotten about buses now she and Neil had a car each. She ignored the instruction to take the third exit at the next roundabout and headed for home.

"Perform U-turn when possible," she was told.

That's exactly what Jennifer intended to do. She was going to revert to the simplicity of her student days. Neil and she had time to spend together then. They hadn't needed to make plans months in advance just to ensure they could spend an important evening together. They wouldn't have booked a fancy seafood restaurant just because it was the place to be seen either, even if they could have afforded it. She wasn't sure why they were doing it now. Neil preferred dressing casually; dinner jackets weren't him. Jennifer liked simple food; minced scallops with exotic spices weren't her thing.

Jennifer tried ringing Neil. His phone was busy. Tony was called next, as he'd be expecting her to arrive any minute.

"Hello, love. Thanks for the anniversary card. Do you have any money on you?"

"Yes, Mum. Sorry, but you did say you didn't want a present."

"We don't, but there's something you could do for us. Get the bus back and spend the evening with one of your friends. I'd like some time alone with your father."

"Mum! Yeah, OK."

She was sure she heard him chuckle before he disconnected.

Jennifer rang the restaurant to cancel the reservation. Even that got complicated. She was told it had already been cancelled. Jennifer shrugged. She'd been right to decide not to go there if they messed up the bookings.

Jennifer rang Neil. "Darling? About the restaurant…"

"Sorry about that, I tried to call but your phone was engaged so I just went ahead and cancelled. I've been thinking, you were right our lives have got so complicated lately that we hardly seem to get a chance to just relax together. Could we just stay in and I'll cook us something simple…"

"Neil, I'd love that and I love you. But you can't cook…"

"Simple, I said. You go and have a bubble bath and I'll come home as soon as I can."

Jennifer put the milk in the fridge, but left the ironing on the floor of the car. She couldn't remember the last time she'd soaked in a hot bath. Usually a quick shower was all she had time for. There'd been no shower in the flat she and Neil had started married life in. There had been a tiny bath that they'd both squeezed into to save on hot water. Neil used to cook for her then, whenever she had worked late.

Usually it was beans on toast. If they were being extravagant, then they'd add grated cheese or a fried egg and share a can of cider. The water grew cool as she remembered the evenings they'd enjoyed without the benefit of cable TV, work brought home and the internet to distract them from each other. Neil came home just as she was wondering whether to get out or add more hot water.

"Would you like me to start dinner now, or later?" he asked.

"Later," she said and turned on the tap. "We don't want to waste all this hot water."

Some time later they went downstairs, wearing only their dressing gowns.

"Cheese or egg on your beans?" he asked.

Jennifer laughed. "Did you remember the cider?"

"Buying that isn't as easy as it used to be. They had pear, mixed berry, organic, alcohol free, extra strong… It was all too complicated, so I gave up and bought this instead." He produced a bottle of champagne.

"Good choice. I like the simple pleasures in life."

5. Pizza For Supper

After they'd eaten Bill said, "You finish the wine. I'll run the bath and sort this lot out."

There wasn't much to do as he'd seen how tired she was and suggested they order pizza and she have an early night. Maria pushed the cork back into the bottle and enjoyed the rest of her glass in the bath, amongst the mountain of scented bubbles he'd created. She was so lucky, despite what people said.

"He seems shifty," was Dad's opinion.

In a way he was right. Bill did shift-work for a security firm.

"He made mistakes in his past, but who hasn't?" she'd asked.

Dad sometimes accused her of being 'a soft touch' because, like Bill, she sympathised with people in trouble and tried to help. Like him she'd been taken advantage of. In Maria's case it was small sums meaning she'd had to shop prudently that week. Bill had been deceived just once but on a far greater scale. He was now working hard to get out of debt and build a future for them both.

Her dog Jock hadn't been keen on Bill. "He's just jealous," Bill said. "Who can blame him? He's had you to himself and doesn't want to share."

He'd said the same about her friends when they'd urged caution. Some claimed they'd seem Bill in 'suspicious' situations. They simply didn't understand about his job. She shouldn't blame them as she didn't either.

"I don't want you worrying about me," he'd told her.

Cherry, her new stepmother, was more positive. "Bill's good looking and very charming."

Maria told herself that wasn't just because Cherry was glad she'd moved out at last. Until Bill had suggested she rent a flat for them both, Maria had never considered she might be in the way at her father's home.

By the time Maria got out the bath, Bill had a warm towel ready to dry her.

"Good idea about having an early night," she said, giving an inviting smile.

"Sorry, I have to go. Didn't I say?" He looked so apologetic. "Staff meeting. The boss has ideas about expanding the business and wants my input."

Maria was so proud. He'd not been working there long and already he was considered important by the manager.

She snuggled into bed and was almost asleep when her phone beeped. The text was from Bill. 'Hello Gorgeous' it began. He always called her that. When he said it, she could believe it was true. 'Managed to get away. Put on something skimpy and be ready for fun. XXX'

That made no sense. He knew she was wearing her nightie and… Maria was suddenly awake. As a message to her it didn't make sense, but it did if her friends were right and Bill was cheating. Hoping there was an innocent explanation she phoned him back.

"What's up, Gorgeous?" he asked.

"Has your meeting been cancelled?"

"No, I'm here now."

"It's just that I got a text from you."

"No! Um no, that wasn't me... My boss asked to borrow my phone. He must have got the wrong number."

His boss wouldn't send a text like that during an important meeting. She'd been a soft touch yet again, Maria realised as she got dressed. This time it wasn't loans to friends who intended to repay her or sob stories from homeless people who really did need the money more than her. Bill had deliberately worked his way into her affections so she'd use her savings to pay off his debt.

Maria slammed the car door and started the engine. Who was she kidding? The debt was probably another lie, just like all the overtime he claimed to do. That talk about protecting her from worry over his job was so she wouldn't know enough to realise when he was lying.

Over the last few months he'd encouraged her to push her friends away, saying their jealousy was destroying her happiness. He'd put distance between her and her father. Dad had Cherry. Maria was alone. She pressed harder on the accelerator. A crash could end her misery.

Then she heard another sound over the engine and her sobs. Jock, sensing her unhappiness, was whining. Maria slowed. It wasn't fair to put his life in danger.

Maria pulled over and took deep breaths. She was almost at what used to be her home and was now Dad and Cherry's house. Perhaps she'd instinctively headed to Dad for comfort? He'd shake his head and mutter, 'told you so' when he heard about Bill. Then he'd ask how he could help and offer to 'sort him out'.

Dad was already on the driveway when Maria pulled up. As soon as she opened the car door, Jock bounded out with a yelp of pleasure and rushed to greet him. After making a fuss of the dog, Dad said, "You caught me disposing of the evidence."

"Evidence?" For a second she thought he meant Bill's dismembered body, but of course Dad didn't know anything about that yet and in any case wasn't any more violent than Jock. Both contented themselves with a warning growl and stern look.

"Cherry had a really busy day and was shattered. I couldn't be bothered with cooking or washing up myself, so ordered pizza."

Maria almost laughed. "Bill did the same, except of course he didn't pay for it."

"Ah. Did you argue about it?"

"No. I got a text he'd meant to send to another woman."

Dad hugged her. "Oh, love. I was so hoping I was wrong about him."

What had she been thinking? That life wasn't worth living just because some shifty bloke had tricked her? Dad loved her. Her dog loved her. Her friends were still her friends. All, in different ways, had tried to warn her.

For now though, there was just Dad… and Cherry.

"How can we help, love?" Dad asked.

"I'd like a bed for the night and a glass of wine. Did you finish the bottle?"

"We did," said Cherry who'd come out to see what was happening. "But I can easily open another and the bed in your room is made."

Maria grinned at her stepmother. Maybe one day she'd find someone as right for her as Cherry was for Dad.

6. No Instant Coffee

Sue's mouth was dry, her breathing shallow and rapid. She could feel her heart pounding, yet the blood didn't seem to be reaching the muscles in her legs. Nearly there, she told herself; a few more steps and you'll be sat with a nice cup of coffee. The delicious aroma seemed to get stronger with every awkward step. She tried to imagine herself sitting comfortably in the coffee shop beneath her flat instead of thinking about the terrifying few steps on the busy street between the lobby at the bottom of her stairs and the door into the shop. It wasn't far and she'd managed it only yesterday. Of course, yesterday she hadn't been on her own.

When she reached the bottom of the stairs she sat on the plastic chair to rest. Walking was difficult for Sue, ever since the accident which had killed her husband and injured her. With the support of a wonderful medical team, she had learnt to walk again. With the support of her daughter, Lorraine, she'd sold her large house and moved into a flat. Lorraine had also helped her learn to cope on her own. No one could restore her the confidence. The day of the accident, Sue and her husband had been out on a Sunday drive. It had been Sue's idea to go somewhere different and explore. The accident hadn't been her fault. She knew she wasn't to blame for the drunk, speeding teenager in a stolen car who lost control on a remote country lane. No one blamed her for the crash. Neither did they blame her for no longer wanting to explore.

Lorraine had moved, with her husband and children, to

23

Kenya. That had been almost six months ago. Sue had gone to the airport with them and they'd drunk coffee together before Lorraine's family boarded a plane and Sue had gone home alone. With Lorraine no longer close, there had seemed little reason for Sue to go out. She hadn't left the flat alone since then. She'd never have the confidence to return to the airport, board a plane and travel to a foreign country.

A kindly neighbour, Lynda, drove her to the shops each week. She helped Sue carry her shopping and would stop at the post office, library or anywhere else Sue wanted to go. It was Lynda who'd provided the plastic chair she was now sitting on.

"No sense you standing out in the cold waiting for me. You can sit in the warm and I'll come and fetch you," she'd said. That had been back in midwinter, but Sue still waited inside even on the hottest of summer days.

Sue wasn't lonely; friends and Lynda visited quite often. She had her books and the television and the long letters she exchanged with her daughter. The last had said, 'I miss you so much, Mum. I must see you soon.' She'd included details of a flight in just a few weeks time.

Lynda had been pleased for her. "I bet you can't wait to see her, and those boys of hers will have shot up, I expect."

That's when Sue had explained she'd lost her nerve to do anything except stay in, or scurry round the shops clutching hold of Lynda's arm.

"You mean that unless I take you, you don't go out at all?"

Sue had shaken her head. "I know it's silly, but the thought of going anywhere scares me. I've got downstairs a few times, but the moment I open the door onto the street, I can't breathe properly and my legs feel weak."

"Oh, what a shame. I know the stairs are a struggle for you, but I can see it's more than that."

"I'd like to go walking with the boys again. We used to go on long rambles through the woods when they were little, before my accident. I couldn't go so far now of course, but it doesn't matter anyway if I can't leave the flat."

"Sue, I don't know what to say…"

"I'm sorry, Lynda. I didn't mean to upset you. It's just that I can't stop thinking about them all the last time I saw them. We were in a coffee shop at the airport, promising we'd all be together again soon." Sue blew her nose and tried to think of something cheerful. "That used to be our thing. Lorraine and I would meet in town once a week for a coffee and a cake. Lovely coffee we used to have, the instant stuff just isn't the same."

"You're right there. The smell from the place downstairs always makes my mouth water. Tell you what; I could do with some now. We could go down there, if it wouldn't upset you to be with me, instead of Lorraine?"

Not wanting to distress her friend, Sue had agreed. With Lynda by her side, she hadn't felt too nervous. Tasting the rich coffee had lifted her spirits. Sitting in the coffee shop with Lynda, Sue had begun to believe she could regain some of her former confidence.

As they'd left their table, the waitress had called out, "Goodbye, hope to see you again soon."

"You could go back, tomorrow," Lynda had said. "You've been in there now, it wouldn't be so strange the next time."

She'd made it seem easy. This morning, Sue had been unable to think of a reason not to try. Now she was sat on the chair, with a dry mouth, pounding heart and shaky legs.

She couldn't do it.

As Sue stood to return to her flat, the door onto the street opened.

"Morning, love," the postman said. He held the door open for her.

After a moment's hesitation, Sue stepped out onto the street, turned left, took two steps and with pounding heart, pushed open the coffee shop door.

"Hello again," the friendly waitress said. She held out a chair for Sue. "What can I get you?"

It was going to be all right. Sue ordered a cup of coffee made from full roasted Kenyan beans. Inhaling the fragrant steam, she smiled; she'd started to conquer her agoraphobia. It was unlikely she'd ever gain the confidence to fly out to Kenya. That doesn't matter as long as she has the courage to take the train and meet Lorraine at the airport when the family fly back for their visit next month.

7. Well Prepared For Christmas

Jo knew she'd bought too much food. Her brother had teased her and her husband, Duncan, about it earlier in the year.

"She goes berserk at Christmas and I just know she'll be even worse now she's got a husband to fuss over," Marc said.

"It's not true!" Jo had protested, not very convincingly. "I like to have all the trimmings, but I don't go berserk. Just because you never bother at all, you think everyone else overdoes it."

"I don't mind if she overdoes things," Duncan had said and patted her head.

"I'm not a kid, you know," she told him.

"Yes you are," both the men in her life said together.

Jo didn't mind the teasing. Marc and Duncan knew about the Christmases she'd missed as a child, because of poor health and a succession of operations. Since she'd been well enough to celebrate however she liked, she'd made the most of every opportunity. Maybe they did have a point, though.

Jo decided to prove her brother wrong and show her husband she deserved better than his slightly patronising assumption she hadn't learned from her previous mistakes. "I won't overdo things, I promise."

"I believe you," Duncan said.

"Me too," Marc added through a smirk.

"Don't be like that."

"Tell you what, Sis. You tell me, hand on heart, after Crimbo that you didn't go completely bananas and next year, I'll do all your shopping and cook you a lavish dinner!" He'd laughed as he left.

Jo had laughed too; Marc's idea of Christmas shopping was to get vouchers for everyone and a bottle of champagne for whoever was cooking his meal.

That had been three months ago.

"Do we really need all this stuff?" Duncan asked looking at the dangerously overloaded trolley on Christmas Eve. "I should have listened to your brother's warning."

"Yes, of course we do," Jo said as she squeezed a tub of organic glacé cherries in the gap between the wheat-free rosemary and sea-salt crackers and the pink grapefruit juice.

"Well, maybe not *need* exactly," she said retrieving the plastic glasses that slithered out.

"But I do like to be prepared for everything. I'd hate someone to call round to see us over Christmas and not having anything suitable to offer them, especially if it was one of your family. I want them to like me."

"They do like you, but even if they didn't then having exactly the right cocktail decoration or snack wouldn't win them over."

"I know. I didn't mean they could be bought. I just want them to feel welcome and you know I like to be prepared."

"You should have been a boy scout," Duncan said, removing the gadget for opening every type of bottle top known to man from her hand and putting it back on the shelf. "OK. We'll buy whatever food and drink you like. I suppose it will all get used eventually. Nothing too weird though and no more corkscrews in case the three we have at home break. Oh, and absolutely no more festive serviettes; we already have at least twenty-seven each for everyone we've ever met."

Duncan said nothing as she selected a bottle of both regular and sugar-free of every mixer the store had. He kept quiet when she bought salted nuts and dry roasted nuts, nuts with the shells on, mixed nuts and raisins and chocolate covered brazils. When she reached the aisle for bottled beers he helped make sure she didn't miss any.

"Gin? Are you sure about that? We never drink gin."

"Your uncle Malcolm said he liked it."

"All right. I suppose we'll need something to go with all that tonic."

Duncan went off on his own when they reached the crisp aisle. Jo looked from his departing back to the overloaded trolley. Perhaps she was overdoing things just for the two of them.

"Load her up," he said when he returned with another trolley.

"Are you sure?"

"I'm sure about the crisps. Any we don't need I can take to work to go with my lunch, so they won't be wasted."

He smiled reassuringly at every selection until they reached the cheese counter.

"Vegetarian cheese? Do we even know anyone vegetarian?"

"Yes, your sister's boyfriend."

"OK," Duncan said.

Jo noted his tone of voice and after accepting the freshly

cut cheese she steered her trolley towards the checkout. She didn't dare look at Duncan's face as the cashier told them the total price. She was still keeping her attention firmly on the trolley when she left the store and heard a familiar voice.

"That's not bad, Sis. I expected to see Duncan following with a second trolley," Marc said after kissing her.

"I'd hate to disappoint you," Duncan said as he caught up with Jo. He was followed by a security guard who was carrying two loaves of bread and a multi-pack of crisps that which escaped en route to the exit.

Marc laughed so hard he needed to hold Jo's trolley for support. Jo glanced at Duncan and they both laughed too, though their chuckles were far more restrained.

"All right if I pop round to see you later?" Marc asked.

"We'll be pleased to see you," Duncan said. "Just as long as you're hungry and thirsty."

Once the shopping was packed away, Jo began wrapping bottles of wine and boxes of chocolates. They were spare gifts, in case they had forgotten anyone. The phone rang and Duncan answered it.

"Jo's got her hands full at the moment, Mum; wrapping presents. I'll put you on speaker phone."

"We've had a fire," his mum's echoey voice announced.

Jo and Duncan began speaking at once, Jo offering sympathy and expressing concern, Duncan asking questions.

"No one was hurt; don't panic. The fire was in the garage, caused by an electrical fault."

"Was there much damage?" Duncan asked.

"The freezer and contents are a write-off. We've also lost

some presents and bottles of drink I had stored in the garage. One of the electric circuits burnt out, so the fridge and cooker are out of action, although we still have heat and light. I've already had a visit from the insurance people and they'll replace everything and get things fixed, although obviously Christmas will cause a delay. I didn't want you worrying about us, but I thought I'd better say something. I expect you'd have called round for a drink tonight..."

"Mum, you were right to tell us. Is there anything we can do?" Jo asked.

"No, it's all in hand."

"Come round here," Jo said.

"For drinks tonight? That would be lovely dear, but are you sure you can manage? Coping with your first christmas as a wife can be difficult enough and there are quite a lot of us. My brother is here and his family and Duncan's sister and her young man."

"It's no problem, you're welcome to come for drinks, but I meant Christmas lunch. You'd need to bring a couple more chairs, but we've got everything else."

"We couldn't possibly..."

"You could, Mum," Duncan interrupted. "Jo means it and she's right, we really do have enough food to go round."

Marc arrived a few hours later. He came into the kitchen to greet his sister and started laughing again.

"What's so funny now?" Jo asked.

"Duncan did tell me to make sure I was hungry, but honestly..." He gestured at the plates of tiny sandwiches, trays of cheese nibbles and bowls of crisps and nuts.

Jo grinned. "Ah! You thought this was all for you? I'm not quite that bad. Duncan's family are coming round for

31

drinks."

Marc helped move the tree to make room for the guests while Jo put a selection of spicy canapés in the oven to warm through. She arranged peppered olives and anchovy wraps and pickled fish around a mound of asparagus spears and artichoke hearts. Maybe Duncan and Marc had a point about her Christmas shopping habits?

Despite her doubts the drinks party was a success.

Uncle Malcolm would have loved a gin, but he was driving. "Good of you to have thought of it though, my dear," he said as he helped himself to more asparagus.

Duncan's sister introduced her new boyfriend who seemed to eat anything without meat in it. None of the items Jo had bought were too obscure for him. He ate at least one of everything, except the cheese.

Marc didn't stay long; Jo knew Christmas parties weren't his cup of tea and appreciated him staying long enough to be polite – and eating plenty of sandwiches and canapés before he left.

Duncan's dad spotted Russian tonic and limes. "Reminds me of a great cocktail recipe I know. I'll make one for everyone if you have any cinnamon sticks and something bright to decorate them with."

There were just enough cherries for the cocktails including two each on the alcohol free versions for the drivers.

As her guests left, Jo repeated her invitation for Christmas Day lunch. They all accepted without hesitation.

The following day, Duncan distributed gifts, including all the spare presents so that, despite the fire, no one went without.

Jo's family called and wished them a Happy Christmas. Marc came on the line, "Just saying hello, the same as I might on any other day. It's very noisy there."

"Yes, you're on speakerphone. Everyone has been wishing everyone a happy Christmas so we've left it set up like that. We have guests; everyone you met yesterday is here."

"Rather you than me, still I hope you enjoy it."

There was almost nothing left to eat by bedtime on Boxing Day. There had been a considerable quantity of food stacked in the fridge and cupboards that morning, but at eleven, Jo remembered she'd invited the neighbours round for a lunchtime buffet. She'd sliced, heated, filled and arranged at record speed. The neighbours had taken a little longer to dispose of her efforts, but they did a thorough job.

"Never mind," Duncan said as he surveyed the empty shelves the following morning. "It would do us good to have something simple today after all the rich food and different beers I've got through. Do we have anything simple?"

While she tried to think of anything she could create from the few remaining ingredients, the phone rang. It was Marc.

"Did it all go OK?" he asked.

"It was wonderful," Jo said.

"If you say so. Sounds like you've not even had time to switch the speaker phone off. Now I suppose you'll be living off mince pies, turkey sandwiches and the unpopular flavours of crisps for weeks. No offence to you Duncan, but I think I'll be avoiding the pair of you until Easter."

"No need," Duncan said. "Your sister is a changed woman. Come round and see for yourself."

When Marc arrived there was no sign of the festive excess he'd seen on Christmas Eve. The decorations that had been removed to make way for guests and trays of food had not been put back up, the gift wrap and empty bottles were already at the recycling centre and the kitchen shelves were almost bare.

"I take it all back, Sis. You really didn't overdo a thing."

"I'm glad you approve. Now stop checking up on me and sit down. I'll get you something to eat and drink."

"A turkey sandwich?" he asked suspiciously.

"Glass of gin and vegetarian cheese on toast?" Duncan suggested, naming the only things he could find.

"Perfect."

"I'm looking forward to Christmas lunch next year as I most definitely won't be overdoing anything then!" Jo said.

"Oh?" Marc sounded even more suspicious.

"That's right," Duncan agreed. "You said if Jo didn't overdo things this time, you'd be doing the shopping and cooking next year. Better forget simple stuff like toasted cheese too. You did promise it would be lavish."

Marc seemed to be having trouble swallowing as he gulped at the gin.

Jo laughed and patted his back "It's OK, I'm only kidding; unless you can think of a use for seventy-six festive serviettes then I'll have to admit I did overdo the shopping."

8. Deadly Drink

Detective Mike Miller was already on scene, where a man's body was slumped across his desk, when his partner Suzy Ellison arrived that Monday morning.

"This is for real then?" Suzy said. "I confess that when I heard our guy was an investment consultant called Buck Moore, I thought someone was trying to be funny."

"The man himself apparently. He was called Charles originally, but changed it when he started trying to make money for American clients as well as British ones."

Suzy noted the strong whisky smell, and that the victim had been fingerprinted. A marker showed something had been removed from the crime scene, immediately below where Mr Moore's hand dangled limply.

"I've done all the preliminaries," Mike told her. "So you can do the easy bit of working out who did it."

"Don't I always?" Suzy asked.

"Yeah, why else do you think we're partners?"

"No one else will work with you!" They grinned at each other as they repeated their regular banter. Suzy knew she was lucky to work with Mike, who was so thorough and methodical. Equally he appreciated her for the way she coaxed information from witnesses and suspects, always seeming to know who was telling the truth.

"His cleaner called us at seven this morning," Mike said. "The doc estimates he's been dead about twelve hours. That paper on the desk is apparently a typed suicide note, in which he admits to embezzling half a dozen people, but I'm not convinced. It's not signed, there's no trace of it on his computer and the paper is quite different from that in his printer."

"So, some of my brilliant deduction skills have rubbed off on you?" Suzy teased.

"It seems so. And no doubt your brilliant skills have allowed you to deduce what's missing from the scene?"

"Judging by the smell, a glass or bottle of whisky."

"Indeed. There was a whisky glass on the floor. It's been confirmed the victim's prints, and nobody else's, are on the glass. I've sent it for analysis, but I'm pretty certain it wasn't just whisky in it."

"Poison?"

"Doc said that's probable. He'll be able to say for sure once he's done a post mortem, but I knew you'd want to see the body in situ."

Suzy studied the scene. "We need to check if he's got a bottle of whisky here and if that contains poison."

"Already done. There's a bottle with un-poisoned whisky and no prints, except one set of the victim's. Mary White must be very thorough."

"The cleaner?"

"Yes. Marvellous woman."

"Made you tea, did she?"

"Yes, and a bacon sandwich. She was a bit shook up, so I sent her home and said we'd be round later. I thought you'd get more from her when she was calmer."

"Good thinking. We'll have a look round here, then go and see her."

A search revealed a list containing, amongst others, all the names on the apparent suicide note. All had figures against them. Mike had begun making investigations into the people listed. So far he'd learned one of the men on the list was dead and the others were very wealthy.

At the cleaner's flat, Suzy asked Mary, "Do you have any idea what happened?"

"Seems obvious. He killed himself."

"What makes you say that?"

"I saw the letter he left. Stole from people, didn't he? Guess he felt guilty for having all that money when others are poor."

"Perhaps. Did he have any enemies, as far as you know?"

"No, nothing like that."

"Not even the people he embezzled from?"

Mary shrugged. "They probably don't know."

"Was he in the habit of drinking whisky in the evenings?"

"Yes, he was. He had other drink for visitors, but if there was just one glass for me to wash in the morning it was a whisky one. Over a hundred and thirty quid that stuff costs!"

"Was he a good boss?"

She looked uncomfortable. "I suppose…"

"Please tell us everything you can. It might help."

"He was alright, but not practical. When I was sick he sent me a whacking great bunch of flowers. Just mess to clear away they were. And if he gives to charity it's things like opera houses and stained glass windows, not people who need it."

"Thank you. That gives me a picture of him. If you think

of anything else, no matter how small or unimportant it seems, please give me or my partner a call."

When Suzy met up with Mike he said, "I've found out more about the people listed in that letter. As I said, one died recently, that was from a long standing illness. One lives abroad and another is on honeymoon with his fifth wife."

"Don't tell me, she's also a fifth his age?"

"Near enough!"

"They were all Mr Moore's clients?"

"Yes. He charged a hefty commission. If he also helped himself to money he wasn't entitled to then it's not something he was about to be exposed for. It's not suicide, is it?"

"You're right – this is murder."

"And the killer is one of the remaining people on the list?" Mike suggested. "Geoff Clark, Martin Hughes or Linda Turner."

"Let's see what they have to say."

Each of the potential suspects were interviewed in turn and asked where they'd been that weekend.

"Poor old Buck," Mr Clark said. "I'd never have afforded my yacht without his help. I was sailing, alone, for the whole weekend. On Friday I went straight from work to the marina, set sail and returned just in time to put my suit back on and drive to work this morning. I often do that."

This was confirmed by the marina staff, but they couldn't rule out the possibility of him having berthed elsewhere and gone ashore during the weekend.

Linda Turner appeared distressed to hear of the death of the man she claimed had made her rich. Her statement was muddled, as she kept remembering more shops and art galleries she'd visited and more people she'd had drinks with that weekend.

"We'll have to try and untangle all that, but even if it's true she might have had time to do it," Mike said.

Martin Hughes took one look at their warrant cards and said, "I suppose it's about the money?"

"What money would that be, sir?" Mike asked.

"The cash I gave poor old Buck on Friday. I say, I'm not the last person to see him alive, am I?"

"You know he's dead then?" Suzy asked.

"It's been all over the TV. Apparently I'm your prime suspect." He cheerfully offered them a drink, gesturing to a selection of bottles including the same brand of whisky which was the last thing Buck Moore tasted. The detectives declined that and cigars, but accepted coffee.

Mr Hughes, smoking the whole time, gave full details of his movements for the weekend, which included long walks with his Great Dane. "I'll give you a list of people I spoke to, but I'm afraid there are gaps. Rufus and I spend a lot of time in the forest on our own."

"The money you mentioned?" prompted Mike. "Did he steal from you?"

Mr Hughes laughed. "Buck? No, he's made me wealthy. It's because of him I can make charity donations. I prefer to do it anonymously, so pay in cash. I'd given him £25,000 on Friday. Isn't that why you're here?"

"Not precisely, sir."

On their way back to the station, the detectives discussed the case.

"Either he lied about the money, or the murderer took it,"

Mike said.

"Yes and I think…"

Suzy was interrupted by a call from Mary. "I saw that Mr Hughes on TV and it reminded me… There was a smell of cigar smoke when I came in this morning. I sprayed lots of air freshener right away, as Mr Moore hated the smell."

The detectives drove straight to her flat.

In the car Mike said, "Any of them could have done it, but the smell of cigar smoke confirms it for me."

"And me," Suzy said. "But the killer doesn't smoke."

On arrival Suzy asked the cleaner to repeat her statement. Then said, "Mary White, I'm arresting you on suspicion of murder. You do not have to say anything…"

An hour later she'd given a full confession. She'd been tempted by the cash she'd seen, so let herself in on Saturday and doctored the whisky. On Monday she brought with her the typed note and replacement bottle of whisky.

"How did you know?" Mike asked Suzy.

"I had my suspicions when she revealed she knew exactly what the whisky cost, as it didn't seem the kind of thing she'd usually buy, but the lie about the cigar smoke confirmed it. There was no such smell when we arrived, and if she'd masked it with air freshener there wouldn't have been any smell of whisky either."

"I was right all along too you know," Mike said.

"Really?"

"Yes – I knew you'd solve the case!"

9. Coffee Break

I was making coffee. My colleague Shaun always expects me to do it and it's best to do what he wants.

"You believe me about my wife's affair, Darren?" Shaun asked when I brought the drinks in.

I mumbled agreement as I righted the chair he'd thrown across the office. I really did believe Lindsay was spending time with another man, but saying so too enthusiastically might set him off.

"So you'll help me catch her out?"

"Why put yourself through it, mate? Just divorce her." I was certain that affair or no affair she wouldn't refuse. He's not the sort of bloke you want to be anywhere near if he's annoyed, and he's often annoyed.

"I worked hard for the big house, and money in the bank; that's why we had a pre nup. If one of us cheats, the other gets the lot."

"But you…"

"Oh, I've had my fun now and then, but that's not the same. There's no evidence against me. I need proof of what she's been up to and you're going to help me get it."

Clearly he thought explaining what he wanted was a compelling reason for me to do it. He reminded me of the school bully who'd put me through hell. Every day Giles had demanded my pocket money, lunch or homework. Usually he tried to get what he wanted by hitting me. Once he put my hand in the bunsen burner flame.

That was over twenty years ago. I can move all my fingers pretty well now, but I still remember what happens if you say no to bullies.

"OK," I told Shaun. "I'll help. You said she visits him in her car?"

The angry purple colour returned to Shaun's face. "I bought her that car and…"

"I know," I soothed. "There could be evidence in there. On Saturday, pretend yours won't go, borrow Lindsay's and meet me so we can search it."

"Hey, that's pretty good. Where do you want to meet?"

"Any guesses where she goes?"

"The coffee shop in town. She's got one of their loyalty cards in her purse."

"I'll meet you outside at ten. Bring a recent photo of her."

As soon as Shaun opened the car door on Saturday morning, I got a whiff of Lindsay's distinctive vanilla scent. We looked through her car, but found no evidence of any affair. Just an umbrella, pack of tissues, bottle of water, change for the car park and one of those flimsy scarves she usually wears.

"Did you bring the photo?" I asked.

It must have been one he'd taken; although beautiful, she looked nervous. "Perfect," I said. "Show it in the coffee shop and ask when she comes in and who with."

"Won't they ask why I want to know?"

"They might… I know, say you're umm, her brother… And you want to treat her and any friend to coffee and cakes as a surprise."

"I'll have to buy a gift voucher then," Shaun said.

"Small price to get this sorted."

He wasn't gone very long at all. "They confirmed it! Said the guy is tall, pale, blond haired and has no distinguishing features. Sounds just like you." He was less calm than when he'd gone in.

"Does this count as a distinguishing feature?" I showed him my scarred hand.

"I never noticed that before."

"I never take a cup of coffee from you."

"That's true. Always get you to make it, don't I?" He shook his head. "She's got me distrusting everyone." He gestured to the sat nav I'd been fiddling with in his absence. "What you doing with that? Even my idiot wife isn't stupid enough to have her lover listed."

"Maybe not, but 'hairdresser' is in there."

"So?"

I swallowed a couple of times. Maybe this was going to be trickier than I'd thought. If I was the one to confirm his suspicions, he might turn his anger on me. I needed him to get mad at the right person.

"Why would she need the address in the sat nav if it's somewhere she goes often? She doesn't have the coffee shop in, does she?"

Shaun selected 'hairdresser' and pressed 'go'. The route which flashed up went to the posh development on the edge of town.

"That's got to be him," Shaun said. "Her fancy man." He started the car and set off in the indicated direction.

"You don't know that," I pointed out.

"Oh, don't I? Who else could it be?"

"A friend?" I suggested.

"Then why not list the address under the right name?"

All the way there I tried to tell him he could be mistaken. The more I said, the more certain Shaun became that he was heading to the home of Lindsay's lover, and the angrier he got.

It was a real relief when he parked outside – even though it was with the nearside wing wedged into the rear of a purple Audi, presumably belonging to the householder. Shaun leapt out and ran up the path.

"Wait!" I yelled, from the safety of the car.

He paused.

"Don't do anything rash," I urged. I'm not sure he heard me, as he'd stopped right by a neatly clipped bush of some kind. Caught in the foliage was a flimsy scarf.

Shaun snatched it and I knew he'd catch a whiff of vanilla scent – if not from the scarf then he'd pick it up once he reached the door.

It wasn't long before Shaun's yelling and banging got a reply. The guy shouted too and took some pushing into the house. I reprogrammed the sat nav, then called the police.

By the time the police had broken in, Shaun was already dead and the other guy didn't look like he'd be far behind. That hadn't been part of my plan, I thought they'd just give each other a well deserved thumping.

I told the officers everything… Everything I wanted them to know, anyway. I proved my identity, gave my contact details and asked for permission to break the news to Lindsay. The request was denied and I spent a considerable amount of time not being very helpful about their enquiries.

I didn't see Lindsay until we met for our weekly coffee.

Yes it was me she used to meet in the coffee shop. No, we weren't having an affair. I met her once at a work function and saw the same haunted look I'd seen in the mirror so many times as a kid. It was clear Shaun bullied her, at the very least, and I'd felt compelled to protect her.

After we'd ordered coffee and cakes, we discussed events.

"I see why he thought I was cheating," Lindsay said. "He was judging me by his standards. I probably acted guilty too, when I went out to meet you. I was so worried he'd find out and hit you."

"That worried me too, especially when the people here described me – but thankfully his suspicions were directed in a different direction."

"That poor man! Why did Shaun think I was seeing him?"

"Because I put his address in your sat nav while Shaun was in here checking up on you. Then when he got to the house he found a scarf like yours outside, and smelled your perfume in the doorway – I'd set the scene early that morning."

"Darren! He did nothing wrong – and I heard he died too."

"Nothing wrong?" I held out my scarred hand. "Giles did this when I was eleven. I was just one of the kids he tortured then and he's been terrorising people ever since. He's been in prison for violent crimes twice and got away with much more." The police initially guessed I was one of his blackmail victims seeking retribution. They didn't give details, but it seemed clear Giles' house wan't paid for by any honest work.

The waitress brought over our drinks and food. "Would you like anything else? Someone left a gift voucher for the pair of you last Saturday, which more than covers this."

I looked at beautiful, gentle Lindsay. A widow now and free to form a relationship if she wanted to. "Shall we keep it for next week?" I suggested.

"Yes, let's."

I stretched my damaged hand toward a coffee mug, finally having closure over the events which caused my injuries – and for the first time accepting a coffee from Shaun.

10. Spice Of Life

"I was thinking that, when Linda and Mark come, we could all go out for a family meal; a nice curry."

Glynnis gripped the phone tightly as she listened to her daughter's plans for the visit. Linda and her family were staying with Helen. Mark and his brood were squeezing in with their fourth sibling Emma. How they'd all fit she couldn't imagine, but they'd manage. It would be lovely to see all the grandchildren together at a happy occasion rather... well, rather than how things had been the last time they were all together. A curry though?

"I don't know, Helen."

"Come with us, Mum. We'll pick you up and bring you home and book it for whatever time you like."

Glynnis wasn't left with any reason to decline, it wasn't as though she'd be doing anything else with her evening. The hospital visits that had taken most of her time were over now.

"Let me think about it."

"Yes of course. Sorry I didn't mean to bully you. It's just... I thought..."

"It's all right, love. I know." She did know; Helen was trying to persuade her mother back to life, to happiness. Glynnis didn't want her children worrying about her. They too had suffered a loss. She glanced out the window in search of a change of topic. "Oh, it's stopped raining. I think maybe I'll go for a walk. The fresh air will do me good."

"That's a good idea, Mum. I'll call you later shall I? See if you've decided about the curry."

"Yes, if you like." Now she really would have to think about it. Think about eating a curry without Nathan.

She might as well go for a walk too. She'd only said it to try to reassure Helen, but the weather really was brightening up and she'd hardly left the apartment in days. Weeks actually, now she thought about it. She'd gone in the car with Helen to the doctor or with Emma to the supermarket, but nothing more.

Glynnis passed the florist's on her way to the cemetery. She'd not realised that's where she was heading until she stopped to wonder if she should take flowers to put on Nathan's grave. She knew what he'd say. "What's the point, Glynny love? I can't see them. Get 'em for yourself instead."

She walked on, empty handed. She was glad it was still too early for the Indian restaurant to be wafting spicy aromas into the air. Glynnis wasn't ready for that.

How many curries had she eaten with Nathan? She couldn't even guess. She remembered many of them though. Especially that first time. She'd been so excited to be asked out by the funniest, cleverest, most charming boy she'd ever met that she'd been even more tongue tied than usual. All she'd been able to do was nod her head.

Glynnis had heard of curry of course, but she'd not tried it. No one she knew had ever tried it, though there had been an Indian restaurant in the town for nearly a year by then. She'd been so nervous she doubted she'd manage to lift the food to her mouth let alone swallow it.

"Something worrying you?" Nathan had asked.

Yes. She was worried she'd be too dull for him, too shy.

She worried that he'd not want to take her out again and her heart would break. Obviously she couldn't tell him that.

"Will it burn?" she managed to croak out.

He'd reached over and squeezed her hand. "Trust me."

At that moment she'd have swallowed molten larva if he'd asked her too and she was blushing as furiously as if she'd eaten a dish of raw chillies.

Nathan ordered her a rich, creamy chicken dish. The taste was unlike anything she'd tried before, but it wasn't hot or unpleasant. In fact it was delicious. So was the bread and rice to accompany it, once she'd accepted them as an alternative to potatoes.

"How about ice cream?" he'd asked once she'd cleared her plate.

"Is that hot?"

He'd laughed at her feeble joke. "It's not, but I reckon I'll having you eating hot curries before too long."

He was right. Glynnis became braver in her food choices and gradually in the rest of her life too. By the time they married she'd had the confidence to speak her vows loud and clear and to persuade her mother to include a few spicy items in the wedding buffet at the village hall. By the time Nathan became ill she had the confidence to insist on bringing in his favourite foods each evening, right up until… But she wouldn't think about that.

"And I won't eat curry without you, my love. Not yet," she said to the mound of earth covering his coffin.

She knew what he'd have replied if he could. "Eat something else then. You're a brave girl now, Glynny, you'll be OK." Glynnis nodded her head and went home, stopping at the florists on the way for a bunch of carnations. It wasn't the same as having them bought for her by Nathan, but they were still pretty.

By the time her daughter called back, Glynnis had her answer ready. "I am looking forward to the family meal you spoke about, Helen. I'm not ready for curry though, not without your dad. Why don't we have Chinese instead? Maybe the kids can teach me how to use chop sticks."

11. Baked To Perfection

"Ready for the footie, love?" Jude asked.

"No, not in this rain," Kiri said. "You can drop me at Mum's on your way and I'll keep her company while the rest of you get soaking wet. Be nice to talk to her, just the two of us."

He grinned. "Lovely idea!"

Usually the extended family watched the match before going round to his Mum's for their Sunday dinner. The small team they supported was coached by Jude and the players were his assorted nephews and their friends.

His mum didn't go to the matches. She cooked for the whole family, timing it so the kids just had time for a quick shower as the adults enjoyed an aperitif before she served. Every week she prepared the perfect roast dinner with crispy roast potatoes, herb flavoured stuffing, a selection of fresh seasonal vegetables and jugs of smooth, rich gravy. This feast was always followed with a proper pudding. Jude's mum was a master at crumbles and pies smothered with creamy custard, brilliant at treacle tart, steamed puddings and trifles. Fools, mouses and fresh fruit salad with cream were always popular too. Lemon meringue pie was her signature dish though. She made two, perfect and identical in every way, to feed the whole family.

Kiri's attempts to cook the dish were very hit and miss. Sometimes they looked OK but tasted bland. Sometimes the flavour was good but the pastry hard or the tangy citrus filling too runny. Quite often the meringue collapsed. Jude always ate it and never once pointed out that it wasn't as good as his mum's.

Seeing his delight at what he thought was his wife's attempt to make friends with his mum made Kiri feel guilty about her real reason for suggesting he drop her off. It had nothing to do with being nice and very little to do with the rain. Kiri hoped catching her mother-in-law off guard and stressed would reveal an imperfection or two. Mum seemed really nice, understanding and supportive but it made Kiri feel inadequate in comparison. If she could discover Mum wasn't perfect after all, she'd feel better about herself and like the older woman much more.

Mum didn't look stressed as she opened the door. "Come in love. Let me take your coat. Tea? Sherry?"

Kiri shook her head. Instead of going into the lounge as she usually would have done she wandered into the kitchen. Prepared vegetables waited neatly on the side, there wasn't a thing out of place.

"You're the perfect housewife." Kiri knew she made the compliment like an insult.

"Have to be, I've never found a way to get my husband to tackle the hoovering."

Was she having a subtle dig at Kiri who split the housework with Jude? "And you're a GP. That's a demanding and important job."

"Being a teacher is too, Kiri."

"Right."

Mum's face showed concern. "Hey, what's wrong?"

"You're so organised. If anyone walked into my kitchen as I was making dinner it'd be chaos. I'd either yell at them to get out or make them peel potatoes, not offer to make tea."

"I have my Sunday routine pretty much worked out now, but it was chaos to start, I assure you." She touched Kiri's arm. "But yes, we are different. Look at the way you help Jude on Scout camps and cheer on at the football. I never do anything like that."

Mum wasn't just putting on a show. She really was that nice, that perfect.

"Can I help here?" Kiri asked. "Then we can sit and have a drink together."

"Kind of you to offer but... well you see I'm a bit of a control freak. I do everything myself because I don't know how to let people help."

"Oh."

"I would like a proper chat though, we've never really done that, have we?"

"No." That was Kiri's fault.

"Actually the pudding is all I have left to do. It was going to be trifle, but perhaps we could have lemon meringue?"

"Yes please. It's Jude's absolute favourite and I never get it right. If I watch you I might learn the secret to the perfect crisp pastry, tangy filling and sweet crunchy meringue."

"Yes, I should think you will. OK, watch me very carefully." She gestured for Kiri to follow her into the garage. Mum opened the freezer and extracted a couple of bought frozen pies.

"You do one and I'll do the other." She handed one box to an open-mouthed Kiri.

Back in the kitchen Mum, with mock solemnity, demonstrated how to open the box and slide the pie into a china dish. Kiri followed her movements exactly. Mum squashed the box flat and put it in the recycling bin. Kiri did the same.

"Almost perfect love, but I like to put it in with the picture facing downwards, just in case anyone happens to glance in."

"Good thinking!" Kiri corrected her mistake.

"The only other thing to do is slide it into the oven when you take the roast out."

"Reckon I can do that."

"I think we deserve that drink now, don't you?"

"Absolutely."

When everyone had eaten and praised the cooking, Mum said, "I have a confession to make."

Kiri did her best to waggle her eyebrows in a way that would persuade her to keep the secret. Mum looked puzzled for a minute and then smiled.

"I had help baking the dessert," she said. "As I have no daughters I've passed on my secret recipe to my darling daughter-in-law."

The two women clinked glasses. Kiri now knew they were now both perfect; perfect friends.

12. Cheesy-Hammy-Eggy

"We could have cheesy-hammy-eggy for supper again tonight, if you aren't fed up with it after all this time?" Eva said.

"It's only been a month."

"Thought you had it all the time in the navy?"

"Oh. Yes. Perhaps not tonight? I thought maybe we'd go out?"

There it was again, that feeling he was holding something back. "OK. Great." Eva filled the kettle, then watched as Ian sliced the tomatoes from top to bottom instead of across the middle. "You're doing..." She just stopped herself from snapping he was doing it wrong and finished with, "a great job."

"Not too many?"

"No. Just right."

At least they agreed on that. A cooked breakfast was a treat they allowed themselves for Sunday brunch and they both liked a couple of grilled tomatoes with it. Ian liked two sausages, a single rasher and his egg turned over so the white was thoroughly cooked. Eva preferred lots of crispy bacon, no sausage and for her egg yolk to be runny, even if that meant a bit of the white might be too.

Eva liked her tea made in a pot. Ian made it in the mugs. Eva sorted clothes by colour before washing them. Ian didn't.

"With the low temperature eco wash we use, it doesn't

matter," he said.

It was true nothing had been spoiled yet, but it didn't seem right to put his burgundy sweatshirt in with her cream, lace blouse.

As Eva made tea, the right way, and Ian dished up their food she tried to focus on the things they did have in common. At one time it seemed to be everything. Ian was on his first naval deployment when they met, and Eva had just started as a cabaret dancer. They'd got on straight away and swapped addresses when, after three days, they both had to move on in opposite directions. They wrote and spoke by phone frequently and met up whenever they could. Sometimes they travelled hundreds of miles for a few hours together, now and again they managed a whole week's holiday.

They'd both agreed their jobs, which were important to them, meant marriage and children wouldn't be a good idea for some time.

"I've seen the strain it puts on my colleagues and seen too many of them get divorced."

"Me too. So we wait? See how we feel in... say fifteen years?"

It had worked well. They'd continued their relationship not because they were committed by a ceremony or mortgage, but because they wanted to. But now Ian was forty and Eva thirty-four. Ian had retired from the navy and Eva, who was moving on from dancing to choreography, no longer toured and they'd moved into a flat together.

The first week had been huge fun. On their first evening she'd cooked him a cheesy-hammy-eggy for tea. He used to mention that as his favourite supper on board ship and she'd replied it was something she loved too. The troupe she'd joined as a teenager had gone to France and they'd tried lots of local food including Croque Monsieur which, due to their linguistic failings they referred to as cheesy-hammy-eggy. One of the good things about doing two shows a day, plus rehearsals, was that she could eat whatever she liked without gaining an ounce.

Ian had enjoyed the meal she cooked him, then they'd gone up to put the quilt cover on. Eva hadn't realised Ian had turned his end inside out first and somehow they both ended up tangled in the material. They'd laughed at the mess they'd made of it.

It was only gradually she began to feel things weren't right. A few days ago she'd cooked cheesy-hammy-eggy again and as he sat down to eat she was sure he wanted to say something. Was it the tablecloth and serviettes, she wondered? After being in the navy that kind of thing probably seemed too fussy. Eva was used to staying in hotels and had got used to a neatly laid table at every meal. She'd thought they both had the same outlook on life, but really they were very different. Once she realised that, she saw those differences everywhere. She bought a newspaper, Ian read one online. He had his money in the building society. Eva had invested in shares. Ian put apples in the fridge. She couldn't eat them chilled.

Mostly it was silly little things, but Eva thought they indicated a bigger issue. Eva's family lived close by and were always popping in or inviting them round. Ian rarely saw his and had never introduced Eva to them. He would have done surely, if he still wanted to marry her? He'd not mentioned that at all since they'd moved into the flat. She hadn't pushed him to set a date as she didn't want to push him away instead.

As she washed up, so she could do the glasses they'd used for orange juice first, not last, Ian dried. When she was on her own she just left crockery to drip but, perhaps because of his time in the navy, Ian didn't like anything left out. It was quite nice to be able to start cooking a meal without first having to put away what they'd eaten the last one off, she'd decided after a few days. Before she could tell herself their differences weren't really a problem, he interrupted her thoughts.

"About supper... Mum and Dad have invited us over. It's a long way to drive just for a few hours though."

Why didn't he want to accept? Was he ashamed of her?

"We used to travel much further than that without thinking twice and sometimes we barely had time for a kiss."

"So, you want to go?"

"Yes." She spoke firmly. Whatever was wrong, she wanted to confront it. That way she had a chance to solve it.

They didn't talk much on the way. Then as they got out the car, Ian said, "I should warn you, I've told them quite a bit about you."

There wasn't time to ask what he'd said as the house door opened and his mum came down the path.

"Eva! At last," she said pulling her into a hug. "We were beginning to think he'd made you up."

Ian's dad was a little more formal, simply shaking her hand and saying, "Welcome to the family."

Whatever Ian had told them it didn't seem to be that he was about to break up with her.

"So, can I buy myself a hat yet?" his mum asked as she poured tea from a pot.

"Mum," Ian whispered in what Eva guessed was an attempt to shut her up.

"I don't know how you put up with him," his mum said to Eva. "Never tells anyone anything."

It was slightly reassuring to know she wasn't the only one from which he withheld things.

"I'm making your favourite for supper, cheesy-hammy-eggy," Mum continued.

"Oh. Great."

Was Eva imagining the lack of enthusiasm in his voice?

As his mum chatted away, dropping more hints about weddings, Ian looked more and more uncomfortable. It was a relief when she went to start cooking and his dad talked about football.

The reprieve didn't last long though as his mum called out, "If you want to escape the footie, come in here and chat to me, Eva."

She could hardly refuse.

In the kitchen Ian's mum was grating a pile of cheese. Eva could see bread under a grill and a pan on the hob.

"What is it you're making?" she asked.

"Cheesy-hammy-eggy. I'm surprised he hasn't got you making it. Loved it onboard ship he did and asked for it at home. I didn't know what it was, but he explained. It's quite easy, don't worry. Just toast bread one side, pile on ham and cheese then grill it. Top the lot with a fried egg. I like mine runny, but Ian…"

"Ian likes it turned over so the white is thoroughly cooked."

"Yes! Oh silly me, of course you know him better than

me these days."

"I don't think so."

"Of course you must. Oh, whatever's wrong? I've said something to upset you? Was it talking of weddings? I didn't mean to rush you, but I want grandchildren and ..." She hugged Eva again. "Oh, I've really done it now, haven't I?"

"It's not your fault," Eva managed to sniff.

Ian's mum produced tissues and Eva blew her nose. "Sorry. It's not anyone's fault. It's just that Ian and I don't really know each other as well as we thought. We're so different. I was hoping we'd get married, but he seems to have gone off that idea and we've never really talked about children."

"There's time for all that. You've only just set up home together. You need to sort out the little things first."

"We're not doing that either," Eva admitted. "The way he slices tomatoes annoys me, but I've never said and I got his favourite meal all wrong. If he wanted us to get married, he'd have told me what it was like, wouldn't he?"

"Only if he wasn't an idiot," Ian said from the doorway.

His mum tactfully left them to it.

"Eva, I'm sorry. When you misunderstood what I meant by cheesy-hammy-eggy I realised we didn't know everything about each other. I'd assumed we thought the same on everything. That, like me, you were eager to get married and start a family. Then I remembered that since the early days we've not talked about that at all."

They held each other for a few minutes, then Eva pulled away and sank down on one knee.

"Ian, will you marry me?"

"Aren't I supposed to do that bit?"

"What does it matter which way we do things, as long as it all comes out right in the end?"

"You have a point."

"So, will you marry me or not?"

"I will!"

They were still kissing when his mum came back in. "So I should look at hats?"

"Yes, you should."

"Good. You go and tell your dad then, and me and Eva will finish up here. Do the salad would you, love?" She passed Eva a tomato and a knife.

"I'll help, then we'll tell him together," Ian said.

Eva cut a tomato his way, from top to bottom and then saw he'd done his right across the middle. They grinned at each other until his mum turned round from the hob to say, "That's not right. You should dice them." The wink she gave Eva suggested the comment was just a joke, or perhaps her way of not taking sides. "Just leave it to me and go see your dad."

13. Cookery Lessons

Amelia snatched up the post, junk mail and local free paper as she came in from a long week at work. She carried the lot into her home office and sorted them. Annoyed at the waste of time she ripped her address details from the unwanted items and shredded them. Then she gathered together everything for the recycling bin. Just as she dropped it in she saw a recipe on the back of the free paper. Gypsy tart; she'd not had that in years! She must buy one next time she was shopping.

Holly picked up the free paper from the doormat after dropping her boys off at nursery school. She flicked through it as she sipped her coffee. When she saw the recipe for gypsy tart she remembered how much she'd loved it at school. She'd make some for the twins. The recipe seemed much simpler than when she and her friends baked it in home economics, but probably she, Amelia and Erin had been messing about so much they'd made things difficult for themselves. Well why not? Erin's messing about had certainly made things difficult later on!

Erin too saw the recipe in the paper. She'd love a slice of gypsy tart, but daren't. It was so fattening with all that pastry and sugar. Maybe she could find a diet version? It wouldn't taste so good, but would be better than nothing. She could do with cheering up after what happened with Lucas. How she'd fallen for him she couldn't imagine. OK so she'd had a crush on him at school, they all had. It seemed she'd not got over it until a few months ago.

What a thing to carry over from school. Why not her friendships, or ability to eat what she liked without gaining an ounce? She could still remember the three of them baking gypsy tart together. The cookery teacher, Mrs Standish, encouraged pupils to get together and cook a meal for their lunch and it was common to invite a pupil, parent or teacher as a guest. Erin couldn't remember what the rest of the meal had been, but she remembered the gypsy tart and that Lucas had been their guest.

Amelia couldn't find gypsy tart in the shops so she bought a treacle one instead. Nice, but not the same. Just as elegant dinner parties with colleagues weren't the same as sharing a bag of chips with Holly and Erin. She missed them and it was her own fault. Not long after they'd left school, Lucas had asked her out. Knowing the other two also liked him she'd kept the relationship quiet and kept her distance from her friends. She'd soon worked out Lucas was a rat, but she had a job she loved by then and somehow never seemed to find the time to contact the girls.

Holly rubbed butter into flour with her fingertips just as Mrs Standish had taught her. She remembered the teacher with great affection.

"Sharing a meal with friends or family is one of life's greatest pleasures," she'd said.

Mrs Standish had clearly thought teaching the ability to do that was far more important than GCSEs. Holly agreed with her. She loved cooking for the twins and she'd loved cooking for Lucas until Erin had stolen him. She'd been saddened when Amelia and Erin drifted away and often wanted to see them again. Now she wished Erin had gone somewhere unpleasant and got stuck there.

Erin gave in and bought ingredients to make a tart. Mrs

Standish had eaten plenty of cakes she remembered and it hadn't seemed to do her any harm. She'd been well past normal retirement age and had been trim, energetic and happy. Erin was none of those things after avoiding fattening food for years; maybe it was time for a different approach?

The following Friday Amelia again picked up the post and the free paper as she came in from work. She'd left on time for what felt like the first time in years. She'd been eating a piece of treacle tart with her afternoon tea when it occurred to her how silly it was that a person whose life was empty other than work hadn't had time to cook such a simple recipe as gypsy tart. What a shame she'd never taken time to try contacting her old friends, or even make new ones. It was time to change and she'd start by cooking herself something nice.

Amelia flicked through the paper hoping to find another recipe. Instead she found an article about Mrs Standish. At eighty years old, she was hosting her own birthday party and would love it if some of her old pupils could come. Amelia immediately phoned the number provided, explained to the reporter that she'd been one of Mrs Standish's last pupils and was eventually given the teacher's contact details.

"It would be lovely to see you, Amelia," Mrs Standish said after they'd exchanged news. "Could you come round before the party so we could have a proper talk?"

"Yes, I'm owed lots of time off work. Would next Monday suit you?"

"Perfect."

Holly too looked through the paper in the hope of finding another recipe, saw the article on Mrs Standish and got in touch to tell her she was putting her cookery lessons to good use feeding her family.

"I would love to see your twins!" her former teacher said.

"They're pretty lively, they might disrupt your party."

"Bring them beforehand then. How about next Monday?"

"I could come in the afternoon when they've finished nursery."

"Perfect."

Erin had been looking for exercise classes when she saw the article. When Mrs Standish suggested Erin visit her on Monday she readily agreed. She could walk there straight after work and start off her fitness programme that way.

Amelia looked on the internet for a gypsy tart recipe, made the dessert and took it with her to Mrs Standish's home. They each ate a slice as they talked.

"I'm so glad your career is going well, my dear," Mrs Standish said.

"Should be, work is practically all I do these days."

"That's a shame. Don't you see your old friends now?"

"No." She explained how once she was dating Lucas she'd lost contact with them. "So silly, especially as he was no good. Can't think what I saw in him now."

The doorbell rang. "Excuse me."

When Mrs Standish returned she was accompanied by Holly and her twins.

"Amelia is that you?"

The girls hugged and Amelia and Mrs Standish made a fuss of the twins.

"I made a gypsy tart to bring, but I'm afraid the boys ate it all," Holly said when Mrs Standish brought out a fresh pot of tea.

"Don't worry, I brought one," Amelia said.

"Great minds think alike!"

The boys played with an antique but sturdy wooden train set as the women chatted.

"This reminds me of the best bit of school," Amelia said. "I remember on rainy days we stayed in the classroom at break time and ate most of whatever we'd made. We were like the three musketeers and you, Mrs Standish, were the king of France!"

"Things have changed a lot since then," Holly said.

"I suppose so, but it'd be fun to get back together again, wouldn't it? You, me, and Erin."

"I never want to see that..." The presence of her sons and former teacher stopped her saying what was on her mind. "I don't ever want to see Erin again."

"Why, what happened?" Amelia asked.

"She stole my husband!"

"No! Erin wasn't like that."

"I didn't think so either, but it seemed Lucas was a lot more important to her than our friendship or the happiness of my family," said Holly.

"I just can't imagine Erin as a man eater."

"Neither can I," Mrs Standish said. "She was always the quiet one."

"They say they're the worst and they're right."

"What happened exactly?" Amelia asked.

"We had some difficulties, Lucas and I, after the twins were born," Holly explained.

"Lucas? Lucas from school?" interrupted Amelia.

"Yes. We got married five years ago. Things were fine until I had the twins. I love them enormously, but caring for them all day was exhausting and I felt I did nothing but change nappies, wash, cook and clean all day. Erin popped in quite often and persuaded me to come round to hers once a week. We only did silly stuff like paint our toe nails and watch rubbish films, but it gave me the break I needed."

"That sounds like Erin."

"It was fine for a while, but Lucas started to get jealous of the kids and the time I spent with Erin. He said I neglected him and I suppose he must have been right. I told Erin I wouldn't be coming round any more until I'd sorted things out with Lucas and I thought she understood. Oh she understood all right. Understood it was the chance to snatch my husband away!"

"Oh, Holly," Amelia murmured.

"Things were really getting on top of me, so one day I left the boys with Mum and went round to Erin's. Lucas's car was outside. I still had her key so I let myself in and found them both in bed."

"No!" Amelia gasped.

The doorbell rang.

"Would you get that, Amelia?" Mrs Standish asked.

"Erin?" Amelia whispered when she opened the door.

"Amelia! How lovely. It's kind of fitting to see you today as I made a gypsy tart the other day." She held up a box containing the last piece. "I've been thinking about you and…"

"Right, good. Let's take it into the kitchen then," Amelia said, steering her friend in the appropriate direction.

"Where's Mrs Standish?"

"In there," Amelia indicated. "You can't go in though. Holly is with her."

"Oh."

"Erin, I can't believe what you did."

"Neither can I. It was so stupid and I should have known she might be upset if she found out."

"Upset? I think someone who finds their friend in bed with their husband is entitled to be more than upset."

"Ex husband, but yeah you're right. I wasn't thinking straight. When Holly said she wouldn't be seeing me I was really hurt. I didn't have anyone but her and I felt so alone."

"I can see that, you've never had much confidence. That's why I can't understand about Lucas."

"It's because of that. He came round to tell me he and Erin had split up. I'd put on weight and was miserable, so when he paid me compliments I just lost my head. I'd always liked him, but of course he'd never noticed me before."

"Lucas told you we'd split up?" Holly demanded from the doorway.

Erin jumped. "Yes. I'd never have let him... you know... if you hadn't." She gasped and stepped back as though she'd been hit. Her mouth flopped open and she stared. "You hadn't? That's why... Oh, Holly."

"If one of you will come and mind these boys, I'll make some more tea," Mrs Standish called.

"Your boys are here?" Erin asked.

Holly nodded.

"Can I just see them?"

"I suppose."

"Aunty Erin!" they shrieked and threw themselves at a leg each.

Holly sat as far away from her as possible and talked to Amelia. Mrs Standish brought in more tea and the rest of Amelia's gypsy tart. Everyone, the boys included, began to eat.

"It's very good, but not my recipe, I don't think?"

"One I found on the internet. A bought pastry case I'm afraid and it said brown sugar and condensed milk for the filling, I thought we used something else?"

"Muscovado sugar and a pinch of cinnamon. It's just as good without though."

"I used cinnamon," Erin whispered. "And low fat condensed milk."

"I didn't leave the cinnamon out either," Holly said. "There is something I'll be leaving out of my life though: my stupidity over Lucas. He'd cheated on me twice before, including while I was pregnant. I was so angry with myself for falling for his lies yet again and desperate for him to prove a good husband and father I tried to convince myself it was Erin's fault, not his. Can I have my friends back instead?"

The three girls left together, heading for Holly's home so they could put the boys to bed and then catch up over a glass of wine.

Mrs Standish waved them off, then cleared away the tea things. She took out her old recipe book and added a note of the changes the girls had made to the version she'd sent in to the paper. Writing those recipes had been such a good idea. It kept her busy and, between regular visits to the newsroom and her old school contacts, she kept up to date with all the gossip about her former pupils.

She wondered if tomorrow's guests would bring a gypsy tart with them, or if they'd have made any changes to her recipe. It didn't matter either way as she'd bake one herself to hold in reserve. Gypsy tart was one of her favourite things to eat and making sure friends continued to share it was her favourite thing to do.

14. Pound Of Flesh

"Gotta run!" my daughter said. She meant it almost literally; her mother and I had agreed if she walked, she could keep the credits it would have cost to use the hoverbus.

Chloe blew kisses, revealing the Fitbit from me on her right wrist. Excellent! She plays Badminton on Fridays and has a powerful smash. It's not favouritism; she wears the ExcyTracker my wife gave her, on alternate days, so it evens out.

I downloaded my daily gym code and left for work. Just like my daughter, I didn't have time to spare. Even so, I hopped off the hoverbus a station before my office, just like the adverts tell us too. I help write them, so I really should take notice. I strode out as fast as I could.

Soon I was hot and sweaty, and all too aware that if I stopped for more than a moment to catch my breath, I was going to be late. Again. You can imagine how relieved I was to recognise one of the homeless guys under the bridge.

I waved to attract his attention and Art raced up the steps to me. "Morning, Gavin."

I gave him my gym code. "You know what to do?"

"Sure. But the kale shake? Must I?"

"It's packed with antioxidants."

He didn't look convinced, so I slipped him twenty credits. Don't judge. Besides, he didn't ask for cash, so technically neither of us were breaking the beggar ban legislation.

I reached the Ministry of Health punctually, so the grim

faces in the conference room weren't because everyone was waiting for me.

"What's up?" I asked the man on my right.

"Rumour has it the research figures have been verified."

I didn't want to believe him, but it was hard not to. Despite all the measures we'd brought in, most of my colleagues were morbidly obese. Heart disease, strokes, diabetes, even gout, were increasing.

I didn't have long to consider the matter though as the meeting was soon called to order.

Our director confirmed the rumour. The poor were now far healthier than the rich, with two decades longer expected lifespan. Problem is their stats haven't improved all that much since the 2020s, whilst ours have dramatically declined.

We, at the ministry, discussed all we'd tried. Our health messages showed before and after all the most popular TV shows, and one appeared and had to be acknowledged for every ten texts sent. I suspected many people just ignored them. We'd reinstated physical education in schools. Some success was reported there, but the benefits needed time to filter through. The 95% cigarette tax helped slightly, but didn't have the impact we'd hoped. The calorie exchange though, how could that be failing?

My wife called at lunchtime. "They've disapproved our grocery order!" she shrieked. "Not enough points."

"Don't blame me. I did a gym session this morning, had the high protein breakfast and kale shake."

"Me too. I don't understand," she said.

"If I have tofu bake and steamed courgetti for lunch, will that do it?"

She took a calming breath. "Not even if I do too. One of us needs to do more exercise. Sorry, but I really, really don't have time today."

It was my turn to take a deep breathe. "OK, I'll sort it out."

"Thank you. I love you, you do know that?"

"I love you too," I said, despite having just proved it.

I took the lift to the office gym. No point using the stairs; Chloe was wearing my Fitbit. I keyed in my code and set the treadmill running. Top speed, maximum gradient, to get it over with as soon as possible.

Man, that thing is boring to watch. I glugged water as I waited. Only an extra five points for that, but it all helps.

Lunch was as awful as I'd feared. I managed to make the tofu halfway passable by covering it in cheese, but nothing could make courgetti worth eating.

Even worse was my wife's text saying, 'Found calorie exchange points problem. Chloe's P.E. class swapped to this afternoon. x'. I'd gone through all that exercise and healthy eating for nothing!

During the afternoon's meeting, my despondency at our failure to do anything to improve the nation's health was brightened by a wonderful thought. With the points from Chloe's Badminton we'd have enough for bacon!

15. Treacle Tart

Kate wasn't really listening as her son talked about his football friends. More of her attention was on the latticed treacle tart she was preparing for them both. She'd probably made it over a hundred times, but it still needed concentration to cut the pastry strips evenly and then weave them neatly together.

She let his chatter wash over her as she worked.

It wasn't that she had anything against football. She'd been glad when Steve started playing the game and hoped it would help him make friends. It had just been the two of them since he was a toddler and she'd worried that put him at a disadvantage. Perhaps she'd over compensated by trying to be a father too. When he said he didn't need her to come to every practise she realised that it wasn't just that other mothers didn't. Not many dads did either. They took it in turns to drive a carload of boys and Steve was welcome to a lift.

Football was good for his confidence it seemed. Or perhaps it was spending time in a male environment which did the trick? Either way she confined her involvement to washing his kit, and cheering from the touchline during competition matches.

He'd continued playing at university. Again she was pleased, knowing it would help him make friends. It would ensure he got some exercise too. Not that she could tell her medical student son much about healthy living. He was the one who persuaded her to add oily fish and whole grains to her diet. He wasn't fanatical though and insisted her treacle tart was a vital food group.

Kate realised Steve had stopped talking and was waiting for a response. What had he just said? Oh yes, something about bringing a friend to Sunday lunch. That was OK, she could roast a chicken and there would be plenty of treacle tart left.

"Your friends are always welcome, you know that."

"Mum, I was telling you about Darren."

Why did he sound so irritated? Kate liked the lad. He seemed such a good influence. Steve told her he gave up the chance of a trial with a professional football team to concentrate on his studies. He still played though, still made time to have fun. Steve tended to become obsessed over one part of his life and neglect the rest. Darren had brought some balance.

"Have you even been listening?" Steve demanded.

"Of course I have." She said that as a reflex. "You were telling me about Darren… You want me to meet him…"

That really was what he'd said, but now she'd finished focussing on assembling the tart she realised it didn't make much sense. She'd met Darren several times. He'd even been to the house at Easter to pick Steve up for a camping trip. Kate had the impression it had been Darren's idea that her son spend at least a few days with her before heading off up a Welsh mountain.

"I want you to meet him properly. Get to know him." Steve's irritated tone was still there.

She'd probably sounded like that herself lots of times in the past when he'd been so absorbed in a game or book that he'd not heard her saying it was time for tea or bed. She shouldn't think about that now though. Concentrate on the present.

"OK. That will be nice. Darren seems... nice."

"He is, Mum. Very nice. He's special."

Kate reached for her pastry brush.

"You do understand what I mean?" Steve asked.

She didn't and it seemed that showed on her face because he raised his hands and gave a strangled sort of cry. Kate knew she'd definitely done the same thing herself when he'd not listened to something important that she'd said.

As she brushed beaten egg glaze over the treacle tart, Kate heard her son going upstairs. She replayed in her head as much of the conversation as she could recall. It was all there, below the surface. It wasn't really that she hadn't been listening. Just as Kate had learned to take a step backwards when Steve was nine and didn't need his mum trailing around behind him at football, she'd tried not to intrude into other areas of his life where she wasn't needed.

Steve had never had a girlfriend. Until about two minutes ago she'd still been telling herself it was because he was shy, he was too busy, he wasn't ready yet. Now she acknowledged what she'd already half known; he never would be ready to meet the right girl. She realised too that he'd been trying to tell her that for some time and she'd, almost deliberately, not heard.

Kate sat down to think. This was nothing to do with him being raised without a dad; it didn't work like that. She'd always done the best she could for her son. He was healthy, clever, kind and hard working so she can't have done too bad a job. She'd always wanted the best for him too. Happiness, a fulfilling career, someone special to share his life with.

She switched off the oven and climbed the stairs to Steve's room. The door was open and he lay on his bed staring at the ceiling. Kate tapped gently and went in.

"I've put the treacle tart in the fridge."

"You don't want to cook it for me now?"

"No. I want to bake it fresh for you and Darren tomorrow. If he's special, your someone special, then he deserves better than leftovers."

16. The Coffee Shop Manager

"Repent of your sins!"

The poor woman was backed up against the library wall as Strange Nigel yelled at her. Margaret, as I knew she was called, was receiving the worst outburst I'd seen from him in some time.

I could see her making placatory gestures and nodding her head. Wisely she wasn't saying anything. I guessed she'd come up against Nigel before. It's almost impossible not to if you come into town on a regular basis, as she does.

I'd only been a local for about three months. It's company policy that promotion to manager means a change of branch and I was lucky to get my first choice. Luckier still to get the position at just twenty years of age. Nigel had been one of the first people to speak to me. Or speak at me is probably more accurate. Forgiveness had been his theme and I'd let him talk for a while, before going in to meet my new staff. I'd been a little concerned they'd resent my youth. Mentioning the encounter had helped break the ice.

"Strange Nigel's harmless enough really, but sometimes he gets worked up and grabs hold of people to try to make them listen. Thing is, he seems to really believe all he says and think he's helping people."

"Usually he just talks."

"Yeah, to himself or the pigeons if no one else will listen."

My experience of him after that agreed with their

opinions. When he was calm he was an interesting and easy person to talk to. He'd been a minister once but illness had forced him to quit. It seemed likely that same illness was the reason for his regularly preaching to a disinterested High Street.

Nigel used the bench outside our shop as his office, so we sort of kept an eye on him. If it was particularly cold, or he seemed especially agitated, one of us took him a coffee and any cakes left from the day before. That always allowed his victim to slip gratefully away.

Margaret, I was sure, would welcome that kind of intervention. "I'm going to rescue her," I told my staff.

One of them made a sweet milky coffee, just how Nigel likes it. "There aren't any stale cakes."

"I'll take a doughnut then." I dropped the money on the counter and set off on my errand.

After Nigel accepted the drink I turned my attention to Margaret. She was pale and it looked like the library wall was being used as a support rather than forming a barrier to her escape.

"Come in and have a coffee," I urged.

She just looked at me so I repeated my offer. She blinked a couple of times. "Oh, it's you."

"Yes. Come into the warm and have a coffee or something. You look like you've had a shock."

"I have. Thank you... Tony."

Although I couldn't bring myself to call her by her name, I was pleased she remembered mine. When I'd told it to her I'd expected it to mean something, but of course it hadn't. That had hurt me. Her unease when I first tried talking to her hadn't bothered me though. She must have wondered what a man, at least fifteen years her junior, wanted from her.

"White no sugar?" I asked once she was sat in a quiet corner. She'd been a regular customer until I'd made too much of an effort to get to know her. I'd learned my lesson. Slightly too late for her to continue using the coffee shop every lunch break, but before she'd stopped talking to me altogether. Once I stopped trying too hard she seemed to like me better and had started coming back in once or twice a week.

I fetched the drink and a couple of florentines; her favourite. "Would you like to talk about it?" I asked as gently as I could and sat opposite.

She shook her head and sipped at her drink. After a minute or so her hand stopped shaking and her skin regained its usual colour. "You heard what he said to me?"

"Some of it, yes. Sounded much like the usual." That wasn't quite true. Repentance is one of his favourite topics, but this was the first time I'd heard him accuse anyone of a specific sin. He'd compared Margaret with the virgin Mary and made it quite clear he considered Margaret to fall well short of Christ's mother.

"There was some truth in it and it gave me a shock."

"Oh. Well we've all made mistakes." I wanted her to keep talking, but didn't want to push her away again.

"That's what it was… a mistake."

"You can tell me if you like."

"Confess?"

"I didn't mean it like that."

"Tony, you seem like a nice lad. You've obviously got something about you to be running this place. Don't waste yourself getting entangled with someone unsuitable."

"Is that what happened to you?"

She gave me a sharp look. "Yes. You said before that you were interested in me and now you want my confession. OK, you can have it." She gulped more coffee. "I was fifteen going on thirty. Pretty and confident and stupid. I let a married man seduce me, the husband of my mother's best friend. I didn't realise I was pregnant until I was several months gone."

"So you had the baby?"

"Yes. A boy. He was adopted."

"That's why Nigel upset you so much? He said something about Mary's devotion to Jesus and you felt bad for giving up your own son?"

"It was the right thing to do, I still think that, but..." She looked up at me. She must have been reassured because she continued. "Yes, Nigel's words upset me, but it was the bit about repentance and forgiveness that did it. Maybe that just makes me more selfish. You see I left a note for him, my son, should he ever ask about me. And I kept social services informed when I moved house. I was hoping that when he turned eighteen he'd try to contact me and I'd be able to explain. I wanted him to forgive me."

"Doesn't sound as though there's a lot to forgive." I meant it.

"I hope he feels that. I hope he's happy." Her tears dropped onto the tablecloth.

"My birthday is the twenty-third of June and I am happy."

"Antony?" Emotions flitted across her face, but I couldn't read them.

I told her that my adoptive family had been wonderful,

81

still were wonderful, and although I'd been a little curious about my birth hadn't felt the need for another mother. I'd read the letter she'd left for me and accepted that she'd done the best thing possible in a difficult situation. It wasn't until the possibility of moving to the town where she lived had come up that I'd decided to find out more about her.

"Now I know why you want to know, I'm happy to tell you everything. I'd like to get to know you too, if you'll let me."

We arranged that she'd come to my flat that evening, then I walked her back, past Nigel, to her place of work.

"Did it work?" Nigel asked as I returned.

"Work?"

"She needed forgiveness. I can always tell."

"Yes, Nigel. She's repented and been forgiven. You need to take your medication though, my friend. You got quite worked up and scared her."

It took some doing, but eventually I managed to persuade him to go with me to the clinic. After that I felt in need of coffee myself and returned to the shop.

17. Biting Her Head Off

Sally wasn't in the best of moods as she unlocked her bakery and switched on the ovens. It was her mother-in-law's fault. Ken's mother sneakily criticised everything she did. She didn't actually come out and say it; Sally could have handled that. They'd have bitten each other's heads off perhaps but it would have cleared the air and they could have moved on. Instead Mum made snide little comments and Sally said as little as possible. A real shame as they used to get on so well before Sally started her business. Now she didn't have time to think straight, let alone deal with Mum's frequent interruptions.

Over the weekend, Sally noticed her hair was suddenly sprinkled with grey.

"Just looks a bit blonder to me," Ken said.

Mum let Sally know she'd noticed by pretending to ask advice on colouring or restyling her own hair.

"I was thinking of letting it grow a little longer," Mum said. "But I wouldn't know what to do with it." She added a little snigger as though laughing off her hint that Sally's untrimmed locks looked a complete mess.

Didn't she realise a woman running a business as well as bringing up children doesn't have time for hours in the salon? Although of course Sally running a business wasn't a good idea, in Mum's opinion, as it meant she wasn't at home to tend to her husband and children. Sally couldn't win there; if Poppy and Daisy spent more than a few hours at Mum's then Sally was neglecting them, if they didn't she was depriving Mum of the chance to see them.

Ken's Mum sometimes offered to cook the girls' tea 'for a change' as though she imagined Sally fed them nothing but cakes. She frequently said it would be no trouble for her to walk down to the school and collect Poppy and Daisy in the afternoons, presumably to save lazy Sally the effort of leaving the shop in the care of her assistant and battling through the traffic.

Despite her disapproval, Mum was a regular afternoon visitor to Sally's bakery.

"I don't know how you resist eating them all yourself," she'd say as she glanced from the tempting cakes to Sally's curvy figure.

Actually Mum bought far more than Sally ate herself, but Mum had plenty of time for walks and Pilates sessions.

Kneading a batch of dough released some of Sally's frustration, but not all of it. She was still feeling bad tempered as she iced a batch of gingerbread men. Smirking to herself she piped on huge buttons to represent Mum's favourite cardigan and a tiny little mouth to form mean little comments.

"You know, you're right, I just can't resist," she said to the biscuit and bit off its head. By the time she'd eaten the gingerbread figure she felt much better.

A few minutes later, Sally thought a regular customer was in a mood as bad as hers had been first thing.

"What's up?" Sally asked.

"My boss is driving me mad," the customer informed her.

"Can you describe him?" Sally asked.

"Really, really annoying!"

"I meant what he looks like," Sally explained.

The customer frowned in concentration. "He looks nice enough. Sort of ordinary really, a bit on the plump side, bit thin on top but nothing you'd call a distinguishing feature except for his ties. He's got lots of different bow ties in garish colours. Why do you ask? Are you going the poison him for me?"

"That wouldn't be good for business, but I have a plan."

When the customer came in the next day, Sally offered her a gingerbread man wearing a bright green bow tie and shiny bald patch.

"Oh! That's Mr McArthur!" the customer said.

"Bite his head of, it'll make you feel much better," Sally told her.

The lady bought the biscuit, and did as suggested. "Delicious, and you're right, I do feel a bit better."

The next day she returned and ordered a dozen. "Everyone in the office wants one, so they can bite his head off just like he does to us."

Soon Sally was baking a variety of biscuits and decorating them to look like unpopular soap characters, politicians and bankers to go alongside a selection of mother-in-laws. They usually sold out by lunchtime.

"I've come early to see your new range," Mum announced one morning. "I've heard you're basing them on annoying people."

"Er yes," Sally agreed.

Mum inspected the gingerbread figures. "Oh, I know who that is… horrible man! And he's the irritating judge on that singing competition and these? Are they… me?"

"Umm…" Sally looked down at the figures of Mum with bright red hair, and yellow and black and green and blue.

"Oh how sweet of you!" Mum said.

"Umm…" Sally repeated, hoping the least said the better.

"Fancy you making time in your busy day to think about hairstyles for me. I think you're right and a dramatic change would be a mistake," Mum said.

Phew!

"Is this one you?" She pointed to a biscuit Sally waving a sugar rolling pin dangerously close to one of the mother-in-law cookies.

"Umm…" Making a few of herself juggling the many demands on her time had seemed like such a good idea.

"You're juggling a rolling pin and a poppy and a daisy! Oh Sally, does that mean what I think it means?" Mum asked.

"Umm…" Sally mumbled.

"We are a pair aren't we?" Mum said. "Me trying to drop hints and you saying it with cakes. Wouldn't it be better if I just came right out and said what's on my mind?"

Resisting another umm, Sally nodded.

"You work so hard. I did just think that if I picked up the children from school and perhaps even had them to stay over once a week it would give you a little more time for yourself and to be with Kenny. As we're speaking plainly, I might as well admit my real motivation is that I'd get to see them more and it'd make me feel useful."

"Oh," Sally said. It hadn't occurred to her that Mum was always coming to see her because she was bored and lonely. "Sounds worth a try. Maybe I'd even get time to have my hair done?"

"I should leave it as it is, love. Those lovely curls and highlights are what made me think of going for something braver myself," Mum said.

"Would you come with me for a minute?" Sally took her out the back, quickly mixed up some icing and piped a scowl onto a gingerbread man. It wasn't much of a likeness, but she knew it was a representation of herself thinking the worst. She handed it to her mother-in-law. "Here, bite the head of this for me, will you?"

"Is this someone who's annoyed you?" Mum asked.

"Let's just say she's someone I want to get rid of," Sally said.

Mum took a big bite and instantly Sally felt much better.

18. Windfall Winners

Joy had put together rather a good tea for herself. Cream cheese and smoked salmon on brown bread and butter, followed by an individual glazed fruit tart. The bread was nice and soft and salmon piled high. The tart was filled with egg custard and topped with blueberries, kiwi fruit and a whole, glistening strawberry. Lovely, although she'd have been just as happy with something less indulgent and someone to share it with.

It was a shame her friend Anthea didn't live closer. They met in the town halfway between them for afternoon tea occasionally, but that treat was becoming ever less frequent. It was two bus journeys for Joy and dear Anthea's knees and pension didn't go far these days.

Joy poured tea into her pretty cup and was just about to add the sugar when her phone rang. She almost didn't bother answering. Anthea had called her only the day before, so was unlikely to be doing so again just yet. No doubt it would be someone wanting to sell her something or saying she was entitled to compensation for something which never happened.

She chided herself for such a negative attitude. It wasn't impossible that one of her family had decided to call. Joy abandoned her meal and lifted the receiver.

"Hello?"

"Good afternoon, is that Miss Joy Chadwick?" asked a female voice.

"It is," Joy admitted. The caller's slightly exotic accent seemed familiar, and they'd got her name and title right.

"I have some good news for you. You've won a prize."

"I have?" Joy was sceptical; she'd received this kind of good news before only to discover she either needed to pay a large delivery fee or attend some kind of sales presentation in order to claim.

"First prize actually, in the Solent Dog Sanctuary raffle."

"Oh goodness!" Now she realised who was calling, Joy recognised the voice as that of the lady who had a charity bric a brac stall in the market. She'd persuaded Joy to buy a book of tickets a few weeks ago. The first prize was a huge amount of money.

"I have your cheque here. I'll put it in the post if you prefer, but I was wondering if you'd mind if I came round and took your photograph, to help with our publicity?"

"That would be quite all right."

They arranged a time for the lady to visit and then Joy rang Anthea. Usually she left it a few days before returning her friend's call, but she didn't usually have such exciting news to share. Five thousand pounds to do with exactly as she wished!

Anthea had been delighted. "That's wonderful, Joy! I'm so thrilled for you."

She reminded Joy of how, as children, they'd fantasised about becoming rich after a neighbour had reportedly done well on the football pools. "We were going to travel and have servants to bring us wonderful food, do you remember?"

"I do! And in those days my winnings would have paid for that," Joy said.

"Ah well, that's progress for you. It might be enough for that walk-in shower you fancied."

"It might, but I'm not going to rush into making a decision just yet, other than to insist you let me treat you to a very special tea the next time we meet up."

"All right, I'll let you pay, but it needn't be anything fancy. It's seeing you and getting out for a change which is most important to me."

After they'd chatted a little longer, Joy brewed a fresh pot of tea and ate her abandoned food. It was all the better for her being a little hungrier than usual, but still not a patch on sharing a plainer meal with her friend.

Joy had agreed with the lady from the charity that her photograph and a report of her win could be passed on to the local paper, but the exact amount of her winnings would not be given. She was quoted as saying she considered the Solent Dog Sanctuary to be doing valuable work. The article also stated that Joy hadn't yet decided how to spend her considerable winnings although some would be used to treat those closest to her.

When her nephew came calling the very next day, congratulating her on her win and hinting that she might like to buy him a new car, she wasn't sure whether or not that had been a good idea.

"The one you have now looks very nice," she said. "At least it does from the outside." Joy had never been in it and only seen it parked outside her house very briefly when he collected birthday and Christmas gifts. He always gave her such beautiful cards, but sadly never had time to stop and talk.

When another relation rang inviting Joy to invest in some scheme of his, she was sure it had been a mistake to agree to any publicity.

"I don't think I want to get involved," Joy told her cousin. "It all sounds so complicated."

"You wouldn't need to do anything. Tell you what, if you're worried about finances you could sign your house over to me and I'll take care of it all for you." He rambled on about equity, ISAs, PPIs, capital and powers of attorney.

Joy didn't understand the relevance of everything he spoke about, but she agreed with his warnings about being very careful what information she gave over the phone and being vigilant so as not to lose her bank cards. "I can see I need to be very careful," she said.

"Exactly. At your age you don't want to be bothered with all that."

Joy ended the call a touch resentfully. She wanted to stay happy about her win, not be made to think of it as a cause for concern. She hadn't been particularly pleased about the reminder of her advancing years and suggestion that made her vulnerable to the unscrupulous either. Thankfully she still had her health and people who cared about her. Joy strode out into the garden. She was just in the mood to tackle the weeds in her rose bed.

"Whatcha doing, Miss Chadwick?" little Charlie next door asked as she attacked the buttercups.

"I'm considering my financial options," Joy said.

"Wassat?"

"I have some money and I'm thinking about how to spend it."

"If I had money, I'd buy 'normous bag of carrots for Tufty." He explained carrots were the guinea pig's favouritest thing.

Charlie's mother called round a few days later. "I'm going down the High Street this afternoon. Would you like a lift, or for me to pick anything up for you?"

"That's kind. I would like a lift thank you."

"Usual time? Congratulations on your win by the way. I hope you're going to get yourself something nice?"

Joy checked the money had been paid into her account, enquired into the cost of cars and value of property in her area. Then she bought cream slices, which were Anthea's favourite cakes. Her basket also contained the scones, cream and jam her neighbour liked and the iced biscuits Charlie was so fond of. Unsure what her relations would most like, Joy selected a range of sandwich fillings. She added a few other essentials and just made it back to the car park at the time her neighbour had said she'd be finished with her own chores.

Joy invited Charlie and his mother to tea the following afternoon. After putting her shopping away, she called her relations, and Anthea, to request they too come for a visit.

Despite his hectic lifestyle, and the short notice, her nephew arrived promptly the following day. With him was Anthea whom he'd collected on the way, at Joys's request. The nephew handed Joy a selection of brochures from car manufacturers and claimed the most comfortable looking of her armchairs.

Anthea presented Joy with a bunch of spray carnations and thanked her profusely for the invitation.

Next to arrive was Joy's cousin, followed closely by Charlie and his mother. When everyone was assembled Joy reminded them all of their suggestions for spending her money. Carrots for a guinea pig, a car, investments and things she herself might enjoy.

"And what have you decided?" her cousin asked.

"To follow everyone's advice. Charlie, go and fetch what's on my kitchen table please."

The boy returned with a huge bag of carrots. "Are these for Tufty?"

"That's right."

"Thank you, thank you lots."

Joy turned to her nephew. "You suggested that I buy a car. Even with my windfall I'm afraid one of these is out of my range," she indicated the brochures. "Besides, except when you think there is something in it for you, no car brings you to see me."

"Oh... I..."

"And, even though she lives near to you and you pass my home on the way to your golf course, it has never been convenient for you to offer Anthea a lift until today. Fortunately the taxi company is most obliging and only requires a very small percentage of my five thousand pounds, so theirs are the only cars I'll be spending money on."

"Did you say five thousand?" her cousin demanded.

"Yes. That's the sum I won."

Joy's nephew and cousin left almost immediately. Charlie and his mother stayed long enough to eat the scones and cakes Joy had provided. The first few minutes were a little strained, but Charlie's chatter soon turned it into a jolly meal.

When only Anthea remained, Joy said, "I didn't finish explaining how I'll spend my money. I'm going to have the most luxurious tea imaginable."

"Oh what fun!" Anthea said. "Where will you go and do you know what you'll have? I'd love to think of you somewhere lovely, being waited on and imagine what everything tastes like."

"No need, Anthea my dear. You're coming too. Those plans we had to travel and be served delightful food are going to come true, for two weeks at any rate – on a cruise."

"Joy, I don't know what to say."

"Please say yes. It wouldn't be half so much fun on my own." It didn't take Joy long to persuade her friend she really meant that.

"I'd love to come. Thank you. Oh, it's going to be just wonderful."

Seeing how shocked her friend was, Joy decided to keep quiet, for now, about her other financial decision. Rather than leave the house to her relations, she was bequeathing her entire estate to the Solent Dog Sanctuary. That wasn't quite as generous as it sounded. In fact they'd be lucky to get much more than the five thousand pounds she'd won from them, as she intended to release the equity in her home to pay for more travel. Perhaps she and Joy would take a cruise, or two, every year. Maybe three. She would certainly arrange a taxi at least once a week, so she and Joy could have tea together.

She couldn't think of any better investment.

19. Salted Shortbread

Robyn was sifting flour when her sister phoned.

"Everything OK?" Serena asked. "You sounded a bit down this morning."

"I'm fine. Just pre-wedding nerves."

"No just about it! You've been a total wreck fretting about things going wrong. I keep telling you, the registrar won't be too sick to conduct the service but if she is they'll send someone else. The bridesmaids won't all get a horrible rash, but if they do I'll trowel on enough make-up that nobody will see. Dad won't break his leg, but if he does he'll hop you up the aisle."

"Have I been that bad?"

"Worse."

"I'd better calm down or it will be me getting ill," Robyn said.

"You won't!"

"I know, I know. And Dominic won't skip the country at the last minute." Mentally she added that there was probably a good reason he seemed to be avoiding her and wouldn't take her calls when she phoned him at work. "I am trying not to panic. Actually I'm making some shortbread."

"Oh! That's good idea."

It wasn't until Serena said goodbye that Robyn wondered if she was the only one jumping to conclusions. Robyn hadn't been thinking of the shortbread trick when she decided to make cookies for the garden birds. Baking always relaxed her and with the wedding less than a week away she needed something to soothe her nerves which didn't carry the risk of making her dress too tight. The bird biscuits would be very bland so she wouldn't be tempted to nibble any; no sugar, not even any salt as that wasn't good for her feathered friends.

Robyn intended to make them in heart shapes with small holes, so they could be hung with ribbons from the trees in her parents' garden. The photographer was coming to the house on the morning of the wedding to take informal shots and the cookies would make the backdrop extra pretty.

As Robyn rubbed lard into the flour she remembered Gran teaching her and Serena how to make shortbread when they were little more than toddlers. That had been the proper kind with butter and plenty of sugar. They'd both been keen cooks ever since; Serena now hoped to earn her living making party food.

When Robyn was sixteen and Serena fourteen, Gran told them she wanted to do something to welcome the new vicar into the village.

"He's been rather a shock to some of the locals as he isn't married. His partner is Scottish so I thought taking round some of my shortbread might be a nice gesture."

Robyn and Serena thought it was a sweet idea until Gran left them with a few biscuits as she went to look for a suitable container in which to package her gift. The sisters eagerly picked up and bit into the top two.

"Urgh! Horrible," Robyn said.

"There's way too much salt and they're really greasy," Serena agreed.

"We'll have to tell her."

"But she'll be so upset. You know she prides herself on her baking."

"I know, but if she gives them to the vicar it'll do the opposite of what she wants. She'd hate that."

When Gran returned with a small cardboard box and tissue paper, Robyn said, "I'm not sure you should give them the biscuits, Gran. They're a bit salty... Perhaps you got distracted when weighing the ingredients."

Gran had smiled. "A bit salty, or totally inedible?"

"Well…"

"We'll help you make some more," Serena offered.

"Bless you both. I tricked you into eating something horrible and you're both only concerned about saving my feelings and helping me out."

"It was a trick?" Robyn asked.

"I prefer to think of it as demonstrating my test. Try another biscuit."

"No thanks, Gran. I think I've learned my lesson," Robyn said.

"Not yet you haven't. Go on, try another."

Both sisters took a tiny bite from another biscuit. Then, once they realised those were as sweet, rich and crumbly as they expected from Gran's shortbread, agreed they'd make lovely gift.

"Thank you, girls. My gift to you is the test. If you're ever not quite sure of someone, reserve a little mixture and work in extra salt and cooking oil for their biscuit. Anyone honest will say it's not very nice. Anyone kind will do it gently."

"So now you know we're honest and kind?" Robyn asked.

"No, you silly girl. I didn't need any test to know that."

Robyn had used the test several times. One boyfriend was very unpleasant about her cookery skills and 'jokingly' warned people not to eat her food. That wasn't the kind of support she'd want in a life partner. Another boyfriend said the biscuit was nice, but didn't finish it. Someone who couldn't face up to anything was no good to her either.

Robyn had suspected a colleague was undermining her efforts at work, taking credit for her good results and wrongly blaming their failures on her. On the day of an important meeting with potential new clients, Robyn brought in some biscuits she'd baked in the shape of the company logo.

"I'll take them in," the colleague offered in her sweetest voice.

Robyn, who had no doubt that she intended to take any praise herself, thanked her. "Could you just try one to make sure they're OK?" She offered the only one which wasn't.

"Delicious," the other woman declared, despite her expression making plain that wasn't true. "You should take them in yourself though and make sure the boss knows this was your idea. It's only fair that you get the credit."

Robyn had done just that and enjoyed seeing the confusion on her colleague's face as everyone enjoyed their refreshments. She'd had considerably less trouble from the woman since. In fact she'd given Robyn this really sweet set of heart shaped cookie cutters as an engagement present. Perhaps Gran's test had done them both good.

She'd never tried the test on Dominic. Although she did sometimes worry about things, his love for her and his kind, honest nature were never in doubt.

Serena had been right that Robyn had felt a bit down that morning. She hadn't seen her fiancé in a week. He'd hardly spoken to her other than to say he was very busy at work, making sure everything would run smoothly whilst they were on honeymoon. He was the manager and very conscientious, but it had felt as though he was making excuses even before he'd cancelled on her that morning. Serena was doing the catering for their evening reception as a wedding present and trail run for the catering business she was almost ready to launch. She'd arranged for them to sample the menu that morning.

"I don't need to try it, I know everything she makes will be delicious," Dominic said.

It was true he was a fan of Serena's cooking but that just made it even stranger that he was turning down the chance to sample it.

Making the special biscuits for the birds wasn't producing the improvement in her mood Robyn had hoped for. She just couldn't shake the feeling something was wrong. Perhaps trying the shortbread test on Dominic would be a good idea. Although she didn't want to discover a problem, it would be better to do so before the wedding than afterwards.

When Dominic did eventually turn up she gave him her biscuit tin. "Help yourself, I'll get the tea."

When she returned with the drinks, he had crumbs on his sweater. "I'm really sorry about the biscuits," he said.

Thank goodness! He was going to tell her, gently, that there were awful and then she could tell him why and they'd sort everything out.

"I was really hungry and I've eaten the lot."

There had been eight in the tin! What on earth could he have done that was so bad he'd rather eat eight disgusting biscuits than tell her the truth?

"Is there something you're not telling me?" she demanded.

He denied it.

Robyn had snapped at him. "You've done nothing but work for over a week! Are you going to bother showing up for our rehearsal tomorrow?"

"Of course I am, love."

Robyn had pushed him away when he tried to kiss her. "Go on, get back to your beloved paperwork!"

Once he'd gone, she'd phoned Serena and then burst into tears. "I can't marry him."

"Don't be an idiot, Robyn. It's just cold feet."

"No, it's more than that."

"If you're really worried try Gran's shortbread test."

"I did. That's the trouble." Robyn explained what had happened.

"I can't believe it. Dominic is such a sweetie. Maybe he actually likes bird food or something?"

"Even if he did, why wouldn't he mention them being different?"

"I don't know, but I'm sure there's a good reason."

"Maybe he's got a brain tumour. That would explain him acting strangely and losing his sense of..."

"Robyn, stop it! Dominic does not have a brain tumour!"

Once Robyn had calmed down she realised she was getting herself worked up over what was probably nothing. Or almost nothing. She agreed with Serena that the rehearsal should help reassure her and afterwards she'd have a proper talk with Dominic.

The wedding rehearsal involved both sets of parents, the bridesmaids, ushers and best man. It went perfectly and Dominic held her hand the whole time and seemed to be looking forward to doing it for real in two day's time. He apologised for being short with her the previous day.

"I was tired," he said.

Before Robyn could reply, Serena invited everyone back to her place for a snack and cup of tea.

"I wanted to talk to you," Robyn told Dominic.

"We'll have time afterwards, or tomorrow."

"No work?"

"No. That's all sorted."

Dominic went to help Serena unwrap food and pour drinks, but quickly reappeared and beckoned to Robyn.

"Try this." He handed her a dainty savoury tart, which had a bite missing. "Only a little bit though, as I think it might be awful."

Robyn tried a tiny amount. It was truly disgusting. Although she glanced towards the kitchen and saw Serena wink, she didn't need that clue to guess what was going on; Serena was using a variation of Gran's test on Dominic.

"You're right, this is awful. Way too much salt. We'd better tell her," Robyn said.

"We can't. She's worked so hard to do all the catering for us. I expect she's tired and made a mistake with that recipe. Understandable, but she'll be really upset if she finds out. You go and talk to her and I'll 'accidentally' knock the tarts on the floor. Then I can throw them away and no one will know."

"She'll be really annoyed with you for spoiling food she's worked so hard on."

"That's better than anyone doubting her abilities, don't you think? If she loses confidence, or people discover she made a mistake, it'll effect her business."

"Yes, but there's no need to worry. The rest of the food will all be fine. Now tell me why you weren't sure if this tart was OK or not."

"There's no time."

"Trust me, Dominic."

He took a deep breath. "It's because I've had a cold. I was worried if you knew you'd panic and think it was the plague, or everyone would catch flu or something, so I just stayed in bed out the way."

So that's why he didn't answer her calls to his office. He was exaggerating, but she supposed she might have worried just a tiny bit. "You are better now though?" Robyn asked.

"Definitely. But my sense of taste is still a bit iffy. Everything's tasted really bland, even those cookies of yours, until I tried Serena's tarts... Come on, we have to stop her passing them round."

"Don't worry, I'm sure the rest will be fine."

Robyn led him into the kitchen where Serena offered him another savoury tart.

"What's going on? Robyn isn't worrying...." He accepted a tart and took a tentative bite. "Oh, it's perfect!"

"Just like you," Robyn said. "And just like our wedding will be – probably. Do you think the youngest bridesmaid is looking a bit pale?"

Serena took the remains of the tart from her future brother-in-law and threw it at her sister. "No, we do not!"

20. Dinner With Aunty

"You're too good to me," I told Aunty over one of her splendid lunches.

"Very true, Jake love. Want to show your gratitude by helping me on the computer?"

"What's the problem?"

"There's no problem, I just need to set up a direct debit and don't want to get caught by some scam or make a silly mistake."

"I can easily do that for you," I assured her. Being cautious is sensible, in fact it was probably me who made her wary of scams. As I work in a bank's fraud department I'm aware how easily people can get caught out.

Aunty's not greedy, so unlikely to fall for scams promising to make her rich and doing the opposite, but she'd be vulnerable to a hard luck story. Sometimes she's just too nice for her own good. She's always helping people out and gets nothing in return.

I helped carry the used crockery into the kitchen, let Aunty talk me into cutting a generous slice of treacle tart to take away, and got her to log into her bank account. As I'd said, setting up the payments was easy. The money was to sponsor a child in a famine stricken country.

"It's not much each month, but will make such a difference to the whole village, not just that little boy," she explained. She was probably right, the charity is well known with a good reputation and the literature's very persuasive.

"OK, that's done," I said. "It's a good idea to check your regular payments occasionally, to make sure you still want whatever you're paying for."

When we looked I noticed she'd apparently written a cheque for five thousand pounds. It seemed unlikely – Aunty is a generous soul, but not extravagant and who writes cheques these day? Worried she was the victim of fraud I asked her about it.

"It's OK, that really was me. I wrote a cheque to help my neighbours. Such a lovely couple."

"Are these the ones you've let take over your garden?"

"No, the other side."

Gently I said, "You should be careful about lending people money. It can cause all sorts of problems."

"I know – that's why I gave it to them."

"You can't do things like that!"

"Yes I can. It's my money."

That was true and I shouldn't have snapped, but I was worried her kind ways would get her hurt when she realised she'd been cheated. Just like I very nearly was.

At work the following week Lynn, the bank's glamorous accounts manager, suggested I take her 'somewhere fun' for the weekend.

"Sorry, I can't. I'm going to my aunty's."

"You said that last time. Not using it as an excuse to avoid me, are you?"

"Certainly not. It's just that I go there every Sunday." That was near enough true, but I did begin to wonder if I was subconsciously keeping Lynn at a distance.

We've been out a few times since I split up with my ex, Clarinda, but don't have much in common. Lynn likes to be taken to the theatre, followed by oysters, champagne and a taxi home. I'm more a pint and the pictures, or dinner at aunty's kind of guy.

"Every week?" Lynn demanded. "What on earth for?"

"Aunty enjoys my company and having someone to cook for," I said.

Again that was true, but she wouldn't mind if I went on a different day and although she'd definitely prefer it to be Clarinda, she'd be pleased I had a date. She'd been none too subtle about her hints it was time I settled down with a nice girl. Trouble was, Clarinda had turned out not to be one and there didn't seem to be many others about.

"I've told you before, you're too nice for your own good," Lynn said, laying a hand on my arm. "Don't let her take advantage of you like that."

Yes, she had pointed out my gullibility before, but this time she was wrong. Aunty didn't take advantage of me. If anything it was the other way round.

"Don't pull that face, Jake. It's just that you seem to be her only relative."

"Yes." Now Mum was no longer with us, Aunty and I were the only close family each other had. She was always ready with practical help and sensible advice and of course she made wonderful roast dinners. It wasn't just those things which made me a regular visitor. I enjoyed her company. She was so optimistic, always looking on the bright side of any situation, forever seeing the good in people – things we'd once had in common.

"So you'll inherit without nearly so much sucking up," Lynn said, proving I was right in my suspicion that although lovely to look at, she didn't qualify as a nice girl.

The next Sunday I went to Aunty's, earlier than usual, to see if I could do anything for her and apologise for snapping over her generosity to her neighbours. I wanted to explain I was simply worried she might have been taken advantage of. She'd not had time to respond before visitors arrived – at the back door.

The neighbours who used her garden carried in loads of fresh veg. From the conversation about various crops it became clear they kept her supplied with garden produce as well as themselves.

"I owe you, and them, another apology for thinking they were taking advantage. I can see it's not like that," I told Aunty once they'd gone.

"No, they're doing me a real favour. They save me paying someone to cut that boring old lawn every week. Now I still get to sit out in the sun when I like, but I never feel guilty for doing that and not weeding or watering."

"Is that the case with everyone you're kind to? You get something in return?"

"Not precisely. Mrs Bridge over the road takes me shopping every week and I don't do anything for her. Perhaps I'll be able to one day, or maybe someone else will."

"I see, but I'm still concerned about you giving people money. They might ask again and it puts you in a difficult position. You should stand up for yourself a bit, ask for something in return."

She gave a mischievous grin. "That's an excellent idea!"

"It is?"

"Yes. You come round for dinner every week, how about you take me out for a meal for a change?"

How could I refuse? Especially as I'd suggested it many times before and so far she'd only accepted on her birthdays.

"Where would you like to go?"

"Quattro."

"I've not heard of that."

"No, it's new. Do you have a date tomorrow?"

I admitted that I didn't, nor on any other day. Oddly she seemed pleased.

"That's settled then. I'll make the booking."

The man who welcomed us in Quattro clearly knew Aunty. He greeted her warmly and showed us to a good table.

"Have I seen him somewhere before?" I asked.

"I expect so. He and his wife are my neighbours. The money I gave them was to help set up this place. They said they'll pay me back and I'm sure they will if they can."

I thought so too, and that maybe she wouldn't have a long wait. The place was very busy for so early on a Monday night. That's why I only caught a glimpse of the waitress.

"Aunty, have you…"

As I spoke I saw that although the similarity was remarkable, the waitress wasn't Clarinda. The woman I'd not only thought was a nice girl but who I'd believed I'd loved and thought loved me in return. That was until I realised she was just scamming me.

The waitress approached with our menus and took our drinks orders. Her gentle manner and musical voice were just like Clarinda's, so much so that I struggled to respond normally.

"That waitress..." I said once she'd moved away. "She looks just like Clarinda. They could be sisters."

"They are."

"What? No, that can't be right!"

"Why not? You told me Clarinda had a sister."

What I'd said was that Clarinda had told me she had a sister. This Merlita was supposedly still living out in the Philippines and allegedly had life pretty tough. Clarinda needed money to bring her over, so she was working extra shifts and wouldn't be able to see me so often as I'd have liked – which back then had been all the time.

Lynn had quickly put me right about that, showing me loads of internet stories where people had got caught out paying to help sick or troubled relatives, on behalf of loved ones, and then discovered those in need didn't exist.

"It's a well known scam, preying on those who are too kind for their own good," Lynn said.

I knew such things happened, me better than many, but that didn't mean Clarinda was involved. I trusted her... But gaining people's trust is how scammers operate. It seemed sensible for me to ask Clarinda a few questions, just to set my mind at rest – and so I could tell Lynn how wrong she was.

I'd phoned immediately. "We need to talk, Clarinda. Can you come round tonight?"

"Sorry, no. I'm working."

"Tomorrow then?" I knew the shop where she worked didn't open late on Wednesdays, but she claimed she'd be working then too.

After I'd ended the call, Lynn said, "I'm so sorry, Jake, but I suspect the reason she can't see you is that she's got other boyfriends she's trying the same game with."

I hadn't wanted to believe that, but once the doubt was planted it niggled away and when eventually Clarinda had time for me, I demanded proof of what she'd told me. The way she'd said nothing in her defence, just walked sadly away, had seemed to prove Lynn was right. Only now, seeing Merlita in the restaurant, did it occur to me that Clarinda hadn't once asked me for money.

"Did you know she worked here?" I asked Aunty.

"Of course."

"You paid for her to come over?" I guessed. Aunty had made no secret of the fact she thought I'd made a mistake over Clarinda. I'd felt that was disloyal. Rather than disagree we'd just not spoken about her since, other than a few unsubtle hints from Aunty.

"No, I didn't. When you told me about Merlita I offered Clarinda help, but the two of you had split up by then. She said it wouldn't be right to take my money and that in any case it wasn't needed as she'd taken on a second job to repay the loan for the flight."

I should have felt pleased Aunty hadn't been scammed. The sensation I experienced wasn't happiness.

"I did help Merlita get this job," Aunty continued. "My neighbours took a chance on someone with no references and she's turned out to be such an asset they say they're again in my debt."

"As am I, for showing me the truth."

"Which is?"

"That Clarinda really did love me. And that I'm an idiot. I

109

worried that I was being too kind and gullible, when I was nothing of the sort. It must have hurt her terribly to discover the man she thought loved her was so cynical and untrusting."

"It did," said that familiar voice by my side. My pint and a gin and tonic were placed on the table. Was it a good sign that Merlita knew about me yet betrayed no dislike? No, not really. She was being pleasant and polite, but then she had a job to keep.

"And do you love her?" Aunty asked.

"I do." I started to tell her how much I regretted my mistake, but soon realised I was talking to the wrong person. Not daring to make eye contact I said, "Merlita, will you tell Clarinda that I'm sorry and I now know how wrong I was?"

"No," she said. "You must do that yourself." Only it wasn't Merlita but Clarinda standing by my side.

Aunty took her gin and left the table.

Clarinda slid into the vacated seat. "Go on then, tell me."

I'm really, really hoping she's too kind for her own good, because if she is there's a chance she'll forgive me and make me far happier than I deserve.

21. Nuts To That

Danielle sang along to the jukebox playing in the bar as she prepared Sunday lunch for hungry customers. The huge beef joint sizzled as she basted it, and the potatoes were a delicious golden brown. She returned the tray to the large oven, took one from the smaller oven and began basting more potatoes.

"You can't do that! Those are for the vegetarian lunches," the landlord told her.

"Don't get your knickers in a twist, George. Potatoes are vegetables aren't they?"

"Yes, but you're using the same spoon as you used for basting the meat."

"So?" Danielle continued to coat the potatoes with herb flavoured olive oil.

"So, people who are vegetarian don't want even the tiniest bit of animal fat on their food."

"What they don't know won't hurt them. I can't be doing with all these gimmicks people come out with. Vegetarian, lactose intolerant, allergic to this, that and the other. They're just being awkward or trying to make themselves seem important."

"No, they're not, but even if they were, that's no excuse. The customer has a right to know what they're eating. You wouldn't try to pass off chicken as duck or serve a well done steak to someone who ordered rare, would you?"

"No, I suppose not." She sighed. "Sorry, of course I

wouldn't."

Danielle put the spoon in the sink, put the potatoes she'd just basted into the main oven and started work on another batch using a clean spoon. "It's just that my son's fiancee won't eat anything I cook. It really upsets me."

"She's vegetarian?" George asked.

"No, allergic to nuts, she says. Jimmy made a huge thing about it. He came in when I was dressing a salad and started asking what oil I was using. When I said I'd made it a few days ago and couldn't remember, he went berserk."

"Berserk? Your Jimmy?"

"Well, OK, I might be exaggerating, but not as much as him. He reckoned if his beloved Jessica was to have a salad with a drop of nut oil in the dressing she'd have some sort of attack. Talk about attention seeking! I said if she wanted to eat in my house, she could take her chances, so now she won't come round, which of course, means I won't see much of Jimmy either."

"Oh dear. It's a shame you've fallen out, but I can see her point of view."

"Oh?" Danielle asked as she peeled carrots.

"Nut allergies can be life threatening. My niece suffers, which is one of the reasons I take care to provide meals for people with special diets."

The following evening, Nancy came into the kitchen as Danielle was making sauce for cauliflower cheese.

"That smells good; what's in it?"

Danielle listed the ingredients. "I used to think you only asked out of interest, but your uncle says you have to be careful what you eat?"

"That's right. Uncle George said you're interested in nut allergies."

"Wouldn't be except my son's annoying fiancée reckons she's allergic."

Danielle drained cooked cauliflower florets and arranged them into individual ceramic dishes as Nancy explained allergic reactions.

"It can be anything from a slight irritation to death."

"Death?" Danielle almost dropped the pan of cheese sauce.

"People who know they have a severe allergy often carry adrenaline injections to try to prevent that."

"Jessica's got one of them," Danielle admitted. She sprinkled cheese over the top of the dishes of cauliflower. "But she wouldn't die if she ate nuts? She'd just use that injection thing and be OK."

"To start with she'd have trouble breathing, then her heart beat would go up and blood pressure down. While that was going on she'd have to remember where she put the pen, find it, then inject herself before she fainted. Without treatment she'd soon become unconscious…"

Danielle put up a hand to stop Nancy saying more. "Last time she visited I'd made a salad and wasn't sure which oil was in the dressing. It could have been walnut and if she'd eaten it…"

Danielle took deep breaths. She filled a glass with water and gulped it down.

Nancy gave her a hug. "I'm sorry I was so blunt, Danielle, but it's awful when people think I'm just making a fuss about my allergy. I was feeling really sorry for this Jessica."

"I'm feeling sorry for her myself now. She could have

died because I jumped to the conclusion she was making a fuss over nothing. Does this run in families?"

"It can." Nancy laughed. "Ten minutes ago you thought this girl was a pain, now you want her to have your grandchildren?"

Danielle shrugged. "If Jimmy loves her she can't be all bad can she?"

"Wouldn't have thought so. Remember, he loves you too."

"Thanks for explaining, Nancy. I'll be able to prepare food that's safe for Jessica to eat and I'll be much more understanding – that's if I haven't left it too late to make friends with her."

"It's only seven o'clock."

"That's not quite what I meant."

"I know it isn't. Go and phone her; even Uncle George must let you take a break occasionally."

Thankful Jimmy had given her the number in case of emergencies. Danielle rang Jessica. She apologised for not being more understanding before.

"I had no idea how serious the allergy could be," she said. "I know now and I promise I'll only cook nut free food when you're there and, well if there's anything…"

"Thank you. Actually there is something you could do."

"Yes?"

"Our wedding cake. I'd love a traditional one, but obviously I can't have marzipan. Jimmy said you might be able to think of an alternative as you're so creative in the kitchen."

"I will. I don't know what, but I'll come up with

something. Will you let me make the cake?"

"Of course. When's your next evening off? I could come round and we could decide on the shape?"

"That'd be great. Now I need to get back to work; we've almost run out of gravy for the vegetarians and I need to make up another batch."

Danielle couldn't go straight back to cooking. Although she doubted anyone would be allergic to her tears of relief, she didn't want them ending up in the food.

22. Spiked!

"I know the last barbie wasn't great," Cathy said.

She was right there. Steve had seen something awful involving her and Stan the fraud, or Stavros the Greek as he preferred to be known. At the time Steve hadn't wanted to accept the image of his wife in the man's arms. He'd tried to believe Stavros's claim he was just trying to help Cathy home, even though he'd been manhandling her in the opposite direction. Steve had been waiting and hoping for an explanation from Cathy, but instead of putting his mind at rest, she'd suggested another barbie, with all the neighbours, just two weeks later!

"I'm sure it will be different this time," Cathy continued.

It would if Steve had anything to do with it. "Any bits in particular you want to change?" he challenged.

"I certainly don't plan to be so ill the day after."

"Hungover more like," Steve said. It was the nearest he could bring himself to mentioning the incident.

"It felt like that, but I was on Pepsi all night."

"Wasn't the charming Stavros plying you with ouzo?"

Cathy shuddered. "You know what he's like. I drank a few drops of the awful stuff in the hope he'd leave me alone afterwards. I was probably ill even then as I can't remember anything after that."

What a fool he'd been! Cathy hadn't been evasive by not mentioning what happened, she hadn't drunk too much, and wasn't a willing participant for whatever Stavros had in mind.

"Come on, cheer up," Cathy coaxed. "It was a shame last month's event wasn't much fun, but it didn't help that you were grouchy – and frankly you have been ever since."

That was true, but with good reason, even if it wasn't the reason he'd thought. He now realised there hadn't just been ouzo in her glass…

"Let's go this weekend, and replace those memories with happier ones," Cathy said.

That, Steve thought, was an excellent idea. He helped set up for the barbie, and chatted to his male neighbours. Steve learned it was common for a woman to be mysteriously taken ill at neighbourhood barbies and Cathy hadn't been the only victim of the last one.

Stavros arrived, just as fake-tanned and smarmy as usual. His Greek accent was as fake and oily as ever, and so was his Greek food. As usual he'd brought the remains of a huge kebab as his contribution to the feast. It was only whatever he had left over from his restaurant the night before, but it was always enough. The meat was as orange and greasy as the man himself. No one ever ate any until they'd drank the ouzo he also brought. The drink, Steve had always thought, was the real deal – the only thing about him which was.

By the time the ouzo was opened there usually weren't many people left wanting to eat. Last month Steve had been one of those who'd not stayed the course. His mind was on work and a presentation he had to prepare – that's why he'd not wanted to go. Cathy had called him a grouch for it. After an hour at home he'd decided maybe she was right and gone back to join her. He'd found her with Stavros.

This time Steve stayed to the end, keeping close to Cathy. When Stavros produced his ouzo, several people called him

Stan, and more than one husband made clear he wasn't welcome. Not Steve – he made very sure not to be seen arguing with the man.

The following morning Stavros was discovered impaled on his kebab spike. The morning sun shining on the blood pooled around his body, looked like the grease collecting under a kebab.

23. Mabel's Memory

"Excuse me, dear," an elderly lady said. "Would you let me buy you and your delightful children some cakes?"

I thought she'd intended to whisper, but my 'delightful' children heard and were looking at me, clearly hoping I'd accept.

I'd been having one of those days. If you've tried clothes shopping with three children you'll know just how I felt.

"Mum, I'm starving. Can we get ice cream?" Tom, my eldest, had asked when we'd been in the first shop for less than ten minutes.

"No," I said. "We have to get your school stuff."

"And Iron Man costumes," Reece said.

"No. Absolutely nothing to do with Iron Man." Not unless it involved me finding my own version of the billionaire hero Tony Stark to pay my bills, defeat the various people who although not true enemies sometimes felt like it, and provide me with either adult conversation or a moment's peace.

"A sandwich then?" Reece suggested.

"No. Now how about these trousers? Do you want to try them on?"

"No."

The word 'no' had come up a lot on all sides. From the older two, to all clothing and footwear which was close to being reasonably priced, washable, and suitable for school.

My youngest, Lucy, didn't say no exactly. She just ignored all my requests to stop running about, or to put things back.

I had already said no, repeatedly, to demands for a mermaid dress, chips, Batman costume, a unicorn (real), burger, Batman boots (despite the shop not selling them), chocolate, unicorn (toy), Batman pyjamas, crisps, kangaroo (real but pink), pizza, Spiderman costume, trip to the beach to look for mermaids, and sushi! Actually I was tempted to say yes to that, in hope the boys would never again request food I hadn't prepared.

"I really, really need a wee," Lucy said.

Some things you just can't say no to, but by then we were in a shoe shop with no customer toilets. I didn't have to ask as I'd explored every inch of the place trying to catch Lucy after I foolishly let her out of the pushchair. Then, when she was safely strapped back in, I'd had plenty of chance for further examination whilst waiting for the poor assistant to fetch pair after pair of shoes, each of which Tom decided were too big or too tight, even before she'd coaxed his feet inside.

"There's a café next door," the assistant helpfully informed me.

Even when she's co-operating, quickly getting a toddler out of her pushchair and on the toilet isn't that easy. Being accompanied by two boys who really don't want to go into the ladies doesn't make it easier. Leaving a four and six-year-old outside wasn't an option. Neither it seemed was getting out without buying cakes which I couldn't afford and they craved.

Mabel, with her request that she be allowed to pay for the treat, seemed like a fairy godmother.

"They remind me so much of my grandchildren and I

never get the chance to treat them these days... Please, do let me."

She was smartly dressed, neatly made up and pleasant looking. The air was scented with rich, reviving coffee. The cakes looked almost as tempting as the squishy sofa by the window. Four pairs of eyes were trained pleadingly on my face. Even without the blister on my left heel, I'd have given the same answer.

"Thank you. That would be lovely."

My children excitedly and very, very politely made up their minds about what they'd like. I requested a latte and shortbread then settled back into the deep cushions. Bliss.

"Here you are, Mabel," the waitress said as she delivered a tray to our table.

I wondered how often she'd done this kind of thing before, to fill the gap left by her absent family. Looking at the huge selection of cookies, tarts and cakes, I felt a twinge of guilt.

Mabel beamed with delight. "So good to see healthy appetites," she said.

I noticed hers was doing OK too. As I nibbled my shortbread she put away a florentine, eclair and most of a cream meringue. Between bites she asked the children lots of questions. They did me proud with the sweetness of their answers and charm of their manners.

"So well brought up!" Mabel praised me. "Young Reece reminds me so much of William."

"Your grandson?" I asked.

Her eyes filled with tears. "No. It's been so long since I saw them that I doubt I'd even recognise them."

She cut through my attempts at comfort. "Ah well, some

older children visit now. I like them and of course there's always little William. We see so much of him on the TV and in the magazines, he feels like part of the family."

"Sorry, I'm not sure who you mean."

"William. Or Wills, but I prefer William." She frowned at me. "Diana's boy?"

"Diana?"

"The Princess of Wales, dear."

"Oh!" I glanced at Reece, trying to recall how Prince William had looked at that age. I couldn't remember, but that was hardly surprising. Mabel's own memory lapse was altogether different and absolutely tragic.

How awful not to realise her grandchildren had grown up, and so miss them even when they came to see her. I assumed they were the older children she'd referred to. Awful for them too. How must they feel when she treated them as strangers?

"Do you go to school?" Mabel asked Tom.

"I do as well," Reece informed her and the conversation became lively again.

Mabel, and the rest of us, remained cheerful until every jam doughnut, cherry slice and chocolate milkshake had been consumed. Then I thanked her for her company. "We really must go now."

"It's been so much fun, thank you so much for inviting me, my dear...

I saw her face cloud with confusion at not knowing my name. I tried to tactfully let her know that not remembering it wasn't something she need worry about. There didn't seem to be a way to correct her about who invited who without causing distress.

The situation was made even more awkward by Mabel loudly telling the waitress, "People are so kind and generous, I really am very lucky."

"You certainly are, love," the waitress agreed.

"Can I have the bill please?" I asked. Although the expense was something I could well do without, the children had enjoyed the meal. Me too, and I was pleased to have brought Mabel some happiness, even if she'd have no recollection of it.

"What are those little cakes with the jam and coconut on and a cherry on top?" Mabel asked.

"Madeleines?" I said.

"That's it! My granddaughter's name and she's very fond of them. Could I have one to take away, please."

I paid for that too.

Mabel was long gone by the time I got Lucy back into her pushchair and informed the boys we had to return to the shoe shop. "That last pair, they were a good fit weren't they, Tom?"

Satiated with carbohydrates, he agreed they might have been.

"Hello again," I said as I manoeuvred Lucy and the boys back into the shoe shop. "Could we just try that pair with chunky laces, again?"

"Oh, yeah sure," she said indistinctly. "Sorry, my gran just brought me a cake and I couldn't resist taking a bite." She wiped a few flakes of coconut from her face and they drifted down past her name badge.

"That was nice of her… Madeleine."

"It was. They're my absolute favourite and she buys me one whenever she's in town. Never forgets!"

24. The Last Ice Cream

Louise stared at the board listing the different flavours. She didn't really need to read them as she knew them all by heart but she could read, thanks to this shop and its owner Luigi Jones.

She'd been coming here for ice creams since she was really small. At first she'd held Mum's hand and pointed at the picture which looked most tempting. Later she'd come on her own. The ice cream shop was just a few doors down from the hairdressers where Mum worked and on the same side of the street so it was quite safe even for a child like Louise who had learning difficulties.

She went when it was quiet because she wanted plenty of time to make up her mind. Louise didn't like to be rushed, but left on her own she got there in the end, whether it was choosing between raspberry ripple and triple chocolate or doing her schoolwork.

Louise enjoyed sitting outside watching the other customers choose. Their eyes sparkled in anticipation of lemon meringue, honeycomb swirl or mint choc chip. She watched their grins as they took that first delicious lick. It was nearly as good as enjoying the sweet, creamy coldness herself.

Luigi started giving her a penny back if she could say which letter her chosen flavour started with. Two pennies when she could spell the whole word. She didn't eat any pistachio parfait, luscious liquorice or marvellous millionaire shortcake for weeks, but Luigi said there were only so many times he'd pay out on 'toffee'. Louise earned another penny if she calculated how much she had to pay after the discount and how much change he owed her. She wanted to get it right every time, not because of the pennies but because of the way he smiled when she did.

"Save them and you can buy another ice cream," Luigi suggested.

"That will take a long time."

"It will, but anything worthwhile always does."

"Then I'll save and save and buy my own ice cream shop!"

Louise didn't need the extra money for ice creams as the lady Mum worked for gave her some for sweeping up hair, washing cups and tidying magazines, so she put it in a jar.

As she got older it was from Luigi she earned her money. At first she just cleaned, fetched and carried, but gradually she learned to serve customers then to order stock and fill in the paperwork. The money he gave her was too much for the jar so she opened a bank account. She filled in the forms herself. It took quite a long time but she didn't make a single error. Luigi had shown her that if she concentrated and if she really wanted to do something, then quite often she could.

Louise loved working in the ice cream shop, seeing the happiness on customer's faces and eating the produce herself, but it seemed she couldn't do that forever.

Other kids laughed at Louise. They said it was stupid to hang around the shop all the time, especially in winter. She should go in the arcades like them. Spend her money on cigarettes and cider. She tried those things, just to see. The arcade machines took her money and gave nothing back, the cigarette tasted awful and made her cough. The cider wasn't too bad but it wasn't anything like as nice as a scoop of rum and raisin or toffee apple crunch.

"Some kids are stupid, but you're not one of them, Louise," Luigi said when she told him her conclusions.

Mum seemed to agree. Louise wanted to prove them both right and worked harder than ever at her studies. She did well enough to earn a place at college. Luigi gave her a double scoop of fruits of the forest when she told him.

That was a few years ago. Louise and her mum had moved away. Her gran wasn't well and they'd lived with her and looked after her until she died. That was sad, but they'd had lots of time to say goodbye and Louise knew Gran wasn't in pain anymore.

"I don't know what we'll do with ourselves now," Mum said.

Louise knew what she wanted. Was it possible?

"You can't just turn back time," Mum said when she tried to explain.

"I know, but we can move back where we used to live can't we?"

The first thing Louise did after unpacking was to race down to Luigi's and order a fudge surprise. The ice cream was as she'd expected, but that was about all. She knew they'd live in a different flat and Mum wouldn't work at the hairdresser's again, but she'd not thought Luigi would be different. He'd got old and was retiring.

"Seventy years this shop has been here. My uncle started it and I carried on. It breaks my heart to think it'll soon be one of those awful arcades or a bookmakers or something else that promises happiness and never delivers."

Louise visited him every day and sampled the clotted cream, salted caramel and banana split. She didn't just eat though; she was working hard, concentrating on her plans. Now it was the very last day that Luigi would serve ice cream and she was to be his very last customer.

"I'm glad it's you," he told her.

"You might not be when you see how I'm paying." She poured a pile of pennies onto the counter.

Luigi grinned. "I remember giving you pennies for learning your letters."

"They're the same pennies, Luigi. I kept them in a jar."

"Really?" He let some trickle through his fingers. "There are a lot. Shame I didn't give you more. You could have bought this place after all."

"You did though. You paid me for my Saturdays and I saved that money too. And then when we went to live with Gran I got a job and saved even more."

"It's you? You've bought this shop?"

"Yes. You've just sold your very last ice cream, but it's not the last one which will be sold here."

"Then let me be your first customer." He scooped up her pile of pennies, lifted the flap in the counter and they swapped sides. He looked up at the board. "It might take me a long time to decide."

"Take as long as you like. The best things are worth waiting for."

25. Just Melt Some Chocolate

"Mum, please would you make me a birthday cake?"

Kara was so busy listening to the first word of Simon's sentence she barely registered what, to him, was the important bit. Her five-year-old stepson had only recently started calling her Mum and it still gave her a warm glow each time. Just before Kara married his father, they'd explained to Simon and his seven-year-old sister they were welcome to address her that way if they wished, but it was their choice.

On her wedding day, Kara had helped Simon with the bow tie on his pageboy outfit and been rewarded with a shy, "Thanks, Mum."

His sister Sasha had hugged Kara and said, "You're as pretty as a fairy princess," which wasn't true and, "So am I," which was.

Both children readily accepted her filling the role of the mother they'd lost and she'd quickly come to love them. They were happy and healthy. Those things were what mattered, not what they called each other, but...

"Mum?"

The warm feeling came again, but this time there was a twinge of guilt too, that she hadn't given him her full attention.

"A birthday cake? Of course, what kind would you like?"

Although Kara wasn't a brilliant cook, she'd be happy to make him a cake and knew he'd love to eat it. She was anticipating, and hoping, he'd request chocolate cake. Pouring melted chocolate over the top of the sponge would produce a neater finish than if Kara were to ice it; she never could get that smooth.

"Dinosaur one, please!"

"Dinosaur? Ah, OK then."

"Thanks, Mum!" He ran off, shouting his good fortune to his sister, no doubt blissfully unaware of the panic he'd caused.

Kara did what so many of us do in this kind of situation and called her own mother. She had more reason than most to do that. Mum had made Kara a fantastic birthday cake when she was about Simon's age. It was an entire mountain with a sugary avalanche actually happening before her eyes. It had been incredible and she'd been especially pleased that it was much better than the plain old Christmas cake they'd cut into the day before. Mum had always made sure her Boxing Day birthday was special and not lost in the Christmas celebrations.

"How can I possibly make a dinosaur shaped cake?" Kara asked. "Once I get to the decorating part I have enough trouble keeping them caked shaped."

"Did you actually promise it would be in the shape of a dinosaur?" Mum asked.

Kara recalled the conversation with a touch of relief. "No."

"Thank goodness for that."

"But I did agree that it would be dinosaur themed and I did say I'd make it, so I don't really think I should buy one."

"No need for that. Just make a normal cake and spread melted chocolate, mixed with cream over the top."

Kara had seen her mum do that, but never considered the reason. "Why mixed with cream?"

"So it's soft, like icing, and easy to slice."

"Ah, right. Double cream?"

"Yes and warm it first."

"I'd better get a pen and paper," Kara said. It seemed as though the instructions were going to get technical.

"You won't need it. That was the trickiest part. Now, I'm assuming Simon still has some of those plastic dinosaurs he got for Christmas?"

"He has. He loves the diplodocus you and Dad gave him."

"That one will be perfect. Make it 'jump' all over the cake, leaving footprints. Say it's where he's been chasing a pterodactyl, which has escaped if you haven't got one, or you can put it on the edge of the plate if you have. Then strew on some malteasers and chocolate buttons as rocks. Flakes can be destroyed tree trunks. Maybe use a squirt of red icing as lava flow…"

"Brilliant, thanks!"

That would be easy to do and the lumps and bumps would hide any disasters such as having to cut off burned bits, which is something Kara had needed to do in the past. All the extra sweets on the top would please Simon, but she wasn't sure about the rest. Kara had been quite excited listening to Mum's description, but once she imagined herself assembling it, she couldn't help thinking it was going to look quite boring, or a bit of a mess. Or both. If only she'd inherited Mum's artistic skills.

Kara did think of adding raisins as dinosaur poo, which she knew would make Simon giggle, but otherwise not improve the situation by much.

Kara shared her concerns with her sister Jacqui.

"Mmmm, a chocolate cake covered in chocolate buttons. I need that for my pregnancy cravings."

"You do not. I know I'm not an expert on the subject, but I'm fairly certain the cravings end with the birth, if not some considerable time before. But if you help me with the cake, I'll let you have a slice."

"Deal. And don't worry so much. Simon and I will love it, no matter what it looks like."

"I suppose, but I wanted to make him something amazing, like that avalanche cake I had when I was seven."

"Or my fab treasure island cake. It had sharks swimming round and loads of treasure."

"I remember! It was incredible. There were palm trees, which had been ravaged by the storm which shipwrecked the treasure hunters, and even part of their boat."

"That was her best, I think, but the elf snowball fight one she did for you was pretty good too. Talking of pretty, do you remember an entire garden with flowers and a swing I had once?"

Kara did remember that. There had been hundreds of flowers in every colour. "Don't you think it's odd she doesn't do anything like that now?" Mum still baked, but not usually anything memorable – unless it was for the wrong reasons. Last week she'd produced a batch of very uneven scones. They'd tasted great with loads of cream and jam though.

And the cake for Dad's retirement was almost entirely chocolate as Kara and Jacqui had arrived while it was in the oven and she'd been so busy talking to them that she'd slightly overcooked it. By the time they'd trimmed off the burned bits it hadn't looked big enough to go round. Undeterred Mum had bought six family bars of chocolate, melted them with cream and built up the cake with the result. She said it represented how sweet their dad was. They'd all loved both that sentiment, and the cake.

"You're right," Jacqui said. "Now I come to think about it, it is strange she didn't do something a bit more elaborate. It's as though she can only make birthday cakes and only for children."

"What difference would that make? I get she deliberately didn't make Christmas cakes special, because of my birthday... Actually I remember one year my birthday cake was house roofs covered in fallen presents because Rudolph had cornered so fast. That could easily have been a Christmas cake, so she could do one if she wanted."

"Maybe it's psychological or something?" Jacqui suggested.

"She hasn't made a special cake since you were about eight. I can't imagine she bought them, can you?" Kara asked.

"No. Fancy cakes like that would be really expensive and it's just not like her to take the credit for someone else's work."

"There must be some secret to making them. I'm going to go over there and persuade her to tell me."

"And I'm coming with you. My little one is growing so fast, I'll be wanting to make birthday cakes myself soon."

After hugs all round, a big fuss over Jacqui's baby, pot of tea with bought biscuits and a catch up on news, the sisters said they were there to find out Mum's cake making secrets.

Dad decided he was needed in the greenhouse and left them to it.

"Come on then, Mum. Is there a trick to it?" Kara asked.

"Yes, I learned it from my own mother. The cakes I made for Jacqui were copies of ones your Granny made for me when I was little, and Kara's were inspired by her Christmas cakes. She told me her secrets, so it's only right I tell you."

The sisters leaned forward a little, eager to catch every detail.

"You simply use lots of imagination, icing and chocolate and don't let anyone over about eight years old see the result."

"There must be more to it than that," Kara said. That advice was even less helpful than the instructions she'd given by phone.

"Yes," Mum conceded. "Depending on the design, you may also need plastic figures, jelly beans, dolly mixtures or marzipan."

"I can see how those things might help, but I still don't understand how to actually do it," Kara said.

"How about the three of us do Simon's cake together?" Mum offered.

"That would be brilliant. Thanks, Mum."

"Sounds like fun, count me in," Jacqui added.

On the morning of Simon's birthday party, the three met up at Kara's home. She already had the cake she'd baked the day before, which she'd accomplished with no disasters. Alongside it was an extremely generous supply of chocolate in different forms and a large pot of cream. Jacqui came armed with more chocolate and a selection of other sweets. Mum's contribution was a bottle of prosecco.

"You got us drunk, Mum!" Jacqui exclaimed. "No wonder we remember the cakes as being fantastic. We could probably see three of them."

"I am not giving alcohol to a bunch of small kids," Kara said.

"No, silly, of course not. This is for us."

As they enjoyed the wine, the women melted chocolate, mixed it with cream and smothered the cake in a thick, gooey later. Before it could set they created the dinosaur footprints and inserted chocolate flakes at jaunty angles.

"They look like the trunks of tree ferns," Kara said. "Shame we don't have anything green for the fronds."

"There were fronds, but Mr Diplodocus ate them," Mum said.

"And then a pterodactyl hatched out of these eggs." Jacqui added white chocolate balls to the top of the cake, eating half of one to add authentic dinosaur hatching damage.

"And the diplodocus chased it all over the rocks," Mum said.

They heaped on the chocolate buttons and malteasers. Some slid off, but Jacqui took care of them, the same way she'd dealt with the white chocolate egg.

Kara confiscated the bag of sweets and discovered licorice boot laces. They reminded her of the vines Tarzan was sometimes shown swinging from. "The cavemen tried to catch him, with these vines," she said, draping them over the toy dinosaur. Now she'd got into the spirit of things she was having fun. Remembering Mum had mentioned lava, she fetched glacé cherries. Pressed halfway in they did seem to be hot bubbles rising to the surface of the chocolate swamp. All the time the three of them were adding to the cake, and the story of the dinosaur, Kara was convinced the cake was wonderful.

Then they stopped, cleared up the mess and she looked at it properly. Although it wasn't boring, the result was otherwise how she'd imagined it would be if she'd attempted it on her own; a bit of a mess.

"Trust me," Mum said and refilled their glasses with the sparkling wine.

Kara took a sip and tried to hide her disappointment. Jacqui took a sip and the last flake.

"Kara, love, one year the birthday cake I'd made you came out really uneven. I was so upset because the Christmas cake had been fine and I thought I was letting you down."

"I don't remember it." Every birthday cake Mum had made her was a total success.

"Ah, but you do, you mentioned it the other day. Anyway, I remembered your Granny showing me how to level it out with extra icing and I did the opposite. That exaggerated the slope."

"My avalanche cake?" Kara guessed.

"Yes. I'd left it all a bit late and put on so much icing, along with a few other bits and pieces, that it really was moving when we cut into it."

"But..." That couldn't be right. In her memory, Kara could still see an entire miniature mountain.

"And the treasure island one got burned on one edge. I cut that bit off to make a beach, put it on a blue plate for the sea and covered it in yellow marzipan for the sand."

"No way," Jacqui said. "There were waves and sharks and

shipwrecked sailors."

"I used lego figures for the sailors."

'And the treasure chest?"

"Made by sticking biscuits together and filled with jelly beans and other brightly coloured sweets."

"And the sharks?"

"You must have made them up yourself. Kara love, you remember how you imagined Simon's cake when I first described it and how it seemed as we were making it?"

"It seemed, well, better…" Much, much better.

"Can you imagine how it would have looked if I'd told you that dinosaur story when you were six?"

Kara could. Her imagination would have turned it into something truly wonderful, just as it had with all the other cakes her mum had made.

When Simon and his friends were assembled, Kara announced that the dinosaur cake was on its way and started telling the children what they'd see. As Jacqui carried it in they were competing with each other to tell their own dinosaur stories. There was only time for a quick and unanimous 'wow' while it was lowered into view before Kara began cutting it up and handing out slices. As they ate ordinary sponge with a lot of chocolate, they were storing up memories of a primeval forest, terrific beasts and a volcano about to erupt.

"I think I understand," Kara said to her mum as they stacked up the chocolate smeared plates. "The brilliance is in their imaginations and stays in their memories."

"That's why I didn't tell you until you asked for my help. I didn't want to spoil those until I had to."

"You haven't done that, Mum. You've replaced them with

new ones; I won't forget the fun we had making and serving that cake."

"Me neither," Jacqui said. "And now I'm imagining you and Granny heaping dolly mixtures onto biscuits arranged like roof tiles, and saying Rudolph dropped the presents, as you guzzled prosecco."

"It was cooking sherry back then, love and I never much cared for that, but we did have a lot of fun."

After Simon's friends had gone home and he'd had his bath, he snuggled up to Kara on the sofa. Although trying to make his birthday last as long as possible, he soon fell asleep and his dad carried him up to bed.

Simon's sister Sasha, who was snuggled into Kara on the other side said, "That was an awesome cake."

"Thank you."

"Really, really awesome. Simon is very lucky."

Kara recognised the hint. "If you like, I could make you one for your birthday."

"That'd be good. Really good. Not a dinosaur one though."

"No, OK."

"Maybe a fairy glen with pixies? Or a princess in a castle with a dragon?"

"Whatever you like, love." Kara wasn't panicking, she still had a couple of months to get Sasha interested in snowy mountains and tell her that a magical princess can ski down an avalanche.

"I can hardly wait to see it… Mum."

Maybe Kara would use white chocolate instead of icing; the warm glow she felt could warm pounds of the stuff.

Thank you for reading this book. I hope you enjoyed it. If you did, I'd really appreciate it if you could leave a short review on Amazon and/or Goodreads.

To learn more about my writing life, hear about new releases and get a free short story, sign up to my newsletter – https://mailchi.mp/677f65e1ee8f/sign-up or you can find the link on my website patsycollins.uk

More books by Patsy Collins

Novels –

Firestarter
Escape To The Country
A Year And A Day
Paint Me A Picture
Leave Nothing But Footprints

Non-fiction –

From Story Idea To Reader
(co-written with Rosemary J. Kind)

A Year Of Ideas:
365 sets of writing prompts and exercises

Short story collections –

Over The Garden Fence
Up The Garden Path
Through The Garden Gate
In The Garden Air

No Family Secrets
Can't Choose Your Family
Keep It In The Family
Family Feeling
Happy Families

All That Love Stuff
With Love And Kisses
Lots Of Love
Love Is The Answer

Slightly Spooky Stories I
Slightly Spooky Stories II
Slightly Spooky Stories III
Slightly Spooky Stories IV

Just A Job
Perfect Timing
A Way With Words
Dressed To Impress
Not A Drop To Drink

Printed in Great Britain
by Amazon